MW01265041

Just say no!

Best wishes,
Barbara Metcalfe

Freeloaders

You never know how many friends you have
until you buy a house in Florida

by

Merle Barbara Metcalfe

authorHOUSE™

1663 LIBERTY DRIVE, SUITE 200
BLOOMINGTON, INDIANA 47403
(800) 839-8640
WWW.AUTHORHOUSE.COM

First published by AuthorHouse 04/13/05

ISBN: 1-4208-2515-1 (sc)

Library of Congress Control Number: 2005900042

Printed in the United States of America
Bloomington, Indiana

This book is printed on acid-free paper.

Dedicated to all my houseguests
(none of whom appear on these pages)

Acknowledgments

I've made my living writing for many years, but when I try to find a way to thank Linda Sebastian adequately, I have a lifetime-first case of writers' block. My patient friend and novel-writing partner is beyond ordinary acknowledgment pages.

Each week we met to exchange the newly-minted pages of our first novels—I looked slyly at her to see if I'd gotten a laugh—again and again she zoomed right in on what needed fixing. She read and proofed for me—more than once—and made the suggestions that gave this book many of its best moments. She encouraged me whenever I decided to quit—and bought me a drink when I won in Orlando—without Linda, this little book just wouldn't be.

Then later in the writing, Pat Johnston joined our little band and provided professional-level editing, and another round of encouragement. What a welcome addition to our small southern Algonquin.

The Florida Writers Association astonished me by awarding *Freeloaders* first prize for humor, unpublished; first prize for adult fiction, unpublished, and Best of Show at their annual conference in Orlando in 2003. I'm so grateful to their organization!

Dr. Suzanne Presley took time from her veterinary practice to make suggestions about Junior's pneumothorax (and explain that to me).

Some loyal friends read early versions and encouraged me—in particular the Dunstall family (my long-time friend Nancy and her parents, Nancy and Donal), the family to whom I owe my happy retirement to Naples. Early on they read and laughed—they don't know how grateful I was for their compliments.

Ottello Bach helped me plot the story line to *Freeloaders.* Some members of the Education for Ministry group at St. Monica's Episcopal Church were early readers (Barbara Myrick even helped me check out some locales), and they continue to inspire me each Tuesday night. The Wednesday Night Clubhouse Quilters, a true sisterhood, were also drafted into reading, and friends that they are, they did so cheerfully even though they'd rather be sewing. Old friends John Cardozo and Fred Thorlin, from my days at Atari, read and critiqued. Ted Suttmeier and Doris Zimmermann, once family and now friends, uncomplainingly read and commented. Each of you gave me good ideas.

And for more years than any of us will admit, Jean and Dick Williams have been in my corner. This abiding friendship has simply graced my life. Church people talk a lot about "unconditional love"—Jean and Dick embody it.

Chapter 1

Charlie, who had long passed the age of wisdom, should have known better than to toe his way up the chain-link fence and hang over the pond to get a better photo. True, his home videos would have been free of the annoying grid pattern the fence imposes on pictures of the animals, but on the other hand, he wouldn't have fallen to his death in the jaws of a dozen furious reptiles.

The crocodiles don't move much in their special pond at the Everglades Wonder Gardens, but they can snap into action in an instant, with 1500 pounds of pressure per square inch as their jaws clamp down over their prey. Or they can drag their intended victim under water where they have more of an advantage. Unlike the alligators, they don't just kill till they're satiated; they kill whenever there's something to kill. But they're deceptive, sunning themselves in their pond, looking like crusty old men enjoying a nap in a row of deck chairs.

The tour guides warn visitors not to hold their children up over the fence to the crocodile pond. "Crocodiles can jump," they tell people.   The hapless tour guide, a young man about 18 years old, carrying a portable microphone, could do nothing for Charlie, at least without lowering himself into the pond and suffering the same fate. He dropped the mike and pushed his way through the crowd toward the office, some 30 feet away. Wonder Gardens visitors screamed and ran or stood stupefied. Animals and birds cawed, squealed, bawled or made every other noise that captive creatures make when something breaks the monotony of their lives.

Karen Sinclair shut her eyes tightly, trying to make the scene go away as the crocodiles thrashed wildly, biting at Charlie and each other in their frenzy to finish him off and their hierarchical struggle among themselves. The camcorder that was the source of the whole disaster lay partly submerged in the fetid water.

"Charlie!" she screamed, finally forcing herself to peer through the fence around the enclosure, seeing what she didn't want to see. She trembled so much she couldn't get a grip on the posts supporting the fence.

The Wonder Gardens attendants ran toward the pond with hooks in hand after what seemed like a long time but probably wasn't. From a distance, they managed to lift what was left of Charlie into a huge net and deposit it, streaming blood and muddy, sulfurous water, onto a stretcher. "Is anyone with this man?" a bearded man with "Curly" embroidered on his Wonder Gardens shirt asked.

Karen stepped timidly toward the group of uniformed attendants and looked resolutely at the figure on the stretcher. He was almost beyond recognition, but it had to be Charlie. She'd seen him lean out past the top of the fence and stretch his camcorder toward the crocodiles. He'd leaned just far enough that his center of balance (a large paunch) was inside the pond, and his toe-hold in the chain-link fence had given way.

"He's my friend," she said, knowing that even if she hadn't witnessed the gruesome scene, the big SHIT HAPPENS on the front of his t-shirt would have been enough to identify him. Karen was embarrassed to be seen with him when they had lunch before their tour, never dreaming that the silly motto would turn out to be portentous.

"Yes, he's visiting from Seattle. His parents are dead, but I can notify his sister. What do I do now?"

"We've called the coroner and the Peaceful Rest Home," Curly told her. The coroner will have to ask you and these other visitors some questions, and then the funeral home folks can take him away and try to clean him up. You can let them know what to do with the, well, the remains."

Karen slumped onto a bench while the attendants found a canvas tarp to place over Charlie. Inchoate thoughts emerged and retreated as she waited. Dread: how would she explain to Charlie's sister, Michelle, what had happened? Revulsion: what could be a more horrible death? Remorse: could she have stopped Charlie before he leaned out into his last fatal dive? Guilt: was she responsible for bringing him to a dangerous place?

And relief: Charlie was due to stay a second week and now he'd be gone.

With the tarp over Charlie, and no more gore to be seen, the crowd retreated, leaving her to her awkward vigil.

"From out of town?" Curly asked.

"I'm year-round here in Bonita Springs," Karen replied. "I came from Seattle two years ago, and Charlie used to work with me at Microsoft. He's—he was—just visiting."

"Damn shame," said Curly.

Karen retired to Naples two years ago, cashing in her Microsoft stock options and leaving the stressful world of high-tech behind. She had little time to enjoy paradise, however, before the winter season began. People she hardly knew were renewing their friendship, professing their eagerness to see her again. They'd love to fly down from their homes in, say, Newark, or Seattle, or Detroit, just to rekindle their ties and relive the old days for a while in January or February. Not knowing how to do otherwise, she always agreed and tried to put some hospitality into her voice.

So, like many other Florida residents so close to the beach, she had a full calendar. The morning one guest left, she'd quickly wash the linens and change the beds in anticipation of yet another guest arriving in the afternoon. She met planes, cooked meals, and ran excursions to the Everglades or the bird sanctuaries or the beach.

Charlie was a friend from her Microsoft days, still employed at the software giant's Redmond campus. An engineer in the Games division, he, too, was counting up a mounting number of stock options. But he decided he needed an escape from the gloom of a Seattle winter with its constant drizzle, cold mornings, and 4:00 p.m. sunsets.

Charlie's visit got off to a difficult start when he insisted on setting up his laptop computer in Karen's small apartment. "I have to check my e-mail," he announced.

"Can't you log on from my machine?"

"And have every hacker in the world reading it? I'm sure you don't have the security I do."

Charlie slept in till 11:00 each morning, following the typical sleep pattern of the software engineer. He didn't want to eat the food Karen had set out, but had to make a grocery store run for Cokes, cheese curls, and M&Ms. During Charlie's first evening in Florida, Karen prepared a meal of the local grouper with fresh Florida tomatoes and avocados.

"You eat a lot of fish?" Charlie asked.

"Yes, this is a favorite here around this part of the Gulf," Karen replied, thinking of the $13.99 a pound she'd paid for the fish that morning.

"They got a Domino's nearby?" he asked. Karen revised the meal planning she'd done for the week. Pepperoni and sausage pizzas would do for Charlie.

They stopped by the video stores to rent copies of the Star Trek movies, "Tomb Raider," and "Minority Report" for the hours after Karen would have gone to bed, before Charlie would begin to be tired.

Charlie didn't have much interest in the beach. Even though southwest Florida was a far cry from a muscle beach, with its retirees and midwestern whiter-than-white vacationers, Charlie was self-conscious about his frame, an encyclopedia illustration of the advanced development of the endomorph. But Karen had managed to drag him out of the apartment for a couple of sightseeing trips, an airboat ride and a swamp buggy ride in Everglades City. Charlie was more interested in tourism if vehicles were involved.

Charlie had missed most of the trip to Everglades City. While Karen drove, Charlie attached a confusing array of cables to his laptop and palmtop and other black navigational devices. "I'm testing three different locational software programs," he announced. He spent the hour-long trip with his head buried in the mass of machinery.

"Alligator on the right!" Karen told him.

"We should be headed more to the east!" Charlie announced, ignoring her. "The GPS…"

"But the road goes this way," Karen pointed out.

"Ah. Yes. We'll come up on an intersection in about 500 feet." He never looked up from his computer to see if he was right.

Karen gave up trying to show Charlie the sights. They could have saved a time, gas, money, and batteries if they'd stayed in her living room where he could comfortably plug in all his devices, for all the scenery he missed She dragged him out of the car at the national park for a brief visit.

He captured a few good close-up shots of alligators in their natural environment, but wanted to get some of the Florida crocodiles for comparison. Since they're dwindling to near extinction in the wild, and Karen had no intention of placing herself anywhere near where one might be found anyway, she thought of the Wonder Gardens with their huge pond of full-grown captive crocs.

And now Charlie's visit was over.

The loudspeaker blared out an announcement, asking the visitors to vacate the park. Refunds would be issued at the desk. A few moments later, the coroner arrived with the team from the Peaceful Rest Home and, unexpectedly, the Bonita Springs newspaper.

"Where is he?" the coroner asked, holding back the breathless photographer, whose usual assignments were bingo games, pancake breakfasts, and rummage sales.

"Over here," said Curly, folding back the canvas tarp so the coroner could see the mangled body. The flash began exploding, and Karen realized she would be part of the pictures for all her friends to see.

"When did it happen?" the coroner asked. No one knew.

"About a half-hour ago," Curly ventured, looking at his watch. It was now 4:10.

The coroner looked Charlie over squeamishly. Most people in southwest Florida died of heart attacks at a very old age. This wasn't Miami, after all. A cursory glance would do to establish that the cause of death was loss of blood. He replaced the tarp quickly and the Peaceful Rest team took over, carrying the stretcher out of the park. Karen followed the little parade to the vans outside.

At the funeral home, Karen phoned Charlie's sister Michelle, in Sunnyvale, California. Karen had met Michelle on a visit to Seattle, so they were slight acquaintances, but of course, Michelle was nearly speechless when Karen told her the story of her brother's misadventure. It was decided that the Peaceful Rest Home would cremate Charlie's remains and ship them to her in Sunnyvale. Karen was thankful that Michelle didn't feel the need to come out to Florida to supervise the disposition of Charlie.

So Karen was free to go home for the evening.

Chapter 2

Although she wasn't much of a drinker, Karen had a full supply of liquor because of the many visitors she'd been entertaining. And this was an evening that called for a stiff drink if there ever was one. She poured Scotch over ice, and put a CD of Mozart's *Requiem* on the stereo as a tribute to Charlie.

Her tuxedo cat, Junior, climbed up into her lap and settled into a loud purr as she stroked his long fur. Junior hid out under Karen's bed during Charlie's visit. Junior was used to a quiet life, and Charlie tended to stomp and speak loudly.

Years before, in Seattle, Karen had found Junior in a gas station. The kitten was covered with oil and completely alone, with cars rolling in and out of the station. She scooped him up in a shopping bag and took him home for a good bath. He responded to her love and care by growing sleek and fat. Now, at nearly 12 years of age, he was still healthy, if a bit slower than the days when he'd race through the house, chasing a feather on a string as long as Karen would last.

While she stroked her beloved cat, Karen reorganized her life. For what was supposed to be the second week of Charlie's visit, she'd canceled all her usual activities. And now a free week lay ahead of her—free, that is before the next houseguest was scheduled to arrive. She could go to the beach alone with a trashy novel. She could call a girlfriend and have a long lunch, or volunteer to serve a meal at the town soup kitchen. She could take in a movie, some chick flick with a teary ending, at matinee rates. All the things she had planned to do in retirement, but now never seemed to have time for.

Revitalized by the prospect of the week ahead of her, she removed Junior to the sofa and bounded to the kitchen. She lined the trash can with a large plastic bag and began to toss things into it—cold pizza slices with congealed cheese and rubbery sausage; sour cream dip, barbecue-flavored chips, and aerosol-can cheese. She hauled the heavy bag downstairs to the dumpster and returned to start on the bedroom. She filled another plastic bag with soggy t-shirts, torn jeans, rubber flip-flops, and graying underwear, which she picked gingerly up from the floor. This would go to Michelle.

Stripping the bed, she found a copy of *Penthouse* under the pillow. She never would have thought it of old Charlie! Protruding from the pages was a snapshot— Charlie posing with a waitress at a Mexican restaurant in Seattle that she recognized. She remembered Charlie interrupting a meal to ask the waitress to take a picture of him with Karen, and then Karen to take a picture of him with the waitress, as if commemorating a milestone in his life, instead of a simple binge of chips and guacamole and enchiladas.

She raced the sheets and towels to the washing machine and started it running. Energized further by the start she had made, she pulled out the vacuum cleaner and ran it over the whole apartment, dusting and straightening pictures as she worked. When everything was shipshape, she was still not really tired enough to sleep.

She took one more tour of her apartment, checking to see that her housekeeping job was finished. She paused by the kitchen that she had cleaned so diligently and found the M&Ms she had bought for Charlie. She couldn't give the half-opened box to the church food drive, she reasoned, so she began to nibble on them, still standing at the counter. Next to them were the cheese curls that Charlie enjoyed so much. How had she missed them when she cleaned up? When she saw with some chagrin that she'd emptied the bag of candy, she started on them. It wasn't long before her hands were covered with yellow powder—she rushed to the bathroom to wash up and saw that her mouth was coated with the same artificial flavoring. "Disgusting!" she thought to herself. Returning to clear the empty packages from the kitchen counter, she opened the refrigerator. There was the avocado that Charlie had rejected. Those things spoil so fast, she thought, slicing it in half and spooning out the soft fruit with a spoon. It would be good with sliced tomato, and actually that would make a good sandwich with a little mayonnaise. Wasn't there some ice cream in the freezer, too?

* * * *

She was awakened the next morning, a sunny Saturday, by the phone.

"Karen! I just saw the paper! What happened?" It was Karen's best friend, Lucy McNamara, a member of Karen's church. While Karen was uncertain what the focus of her retirement should be, Lucy was clear in her goal of singing professionally. Having already successfully tried out for the Naples Philharmonic Chorale, she gave piano and voice lessons. Lucy lived on a shoestring, never sure if her income would cover the rent, but absolutely focused on music.

"I was planning to call you," Karen replied sleepily. "How about breakfast in a half-hour?"

"I don't know if I can wait that long! I'll pick you up. I don't have any lessons until late this afternoon, and this kid usually cancels anyway—at the last minute."

Karen retrieved the morning paper from her front door mat. She found herself on page one, beside the gruesome body of Charlie, with his t-shirt motto clearly readable. In spite of the sunglasses, her expression was also clearly readable: "Get me out of here." She was

12

clutching her purse as if to protect it from the crocodiles that had lately devoured most of her friend.

Karen looked at the picture of herself in the paper—trying to be objective about the person she saw. She had medium blond hair, tending toward brown, and blue eyes—she often wished for more contrast in her coloring, envying Lucy, whose auburn hair and brown eyes stood out dramatically. The black-and-white photo, however, revealed her expression of shock as clearly as if she'd been wearing stage makeup. Karen was tall and kept her weight under control only with bouts of the most extreme dieting—in the picture, wearing the medium-length shorts outfits she favored in Florida, she looked trim and fit for someone pushing 40 as closely as she was.

The story was the most sensational to hit Bonita Springs since a shark attack off Fort Myers Beach some years back. The reporter dragged out words she hadn't been able to use in years of working for the small-town paper: "devastating," "monstrous," "frenzied," and "horrifying."

Over bagels and tea, Karen told Lucy the story of the day's event. "One minute I saw him climbing the wall, and the next minute, the most terrible sounds—crashing, Charlie screaming for just a moment, and the crocodile jaws snapping. You know, I remembered later that the guide told us that when they snap their jaws shut, you hear a cracking sound, and you think it's teeth, but they're actually breaking the sound barrier."

Lucy shuddered. "How close were you and Charlie?"

"Not very," Karen told her. "We worked together in the Games Division at Microsoft. I had such a hard time understanding the games that I really needed him. I kind of kissed up to him to get him to help me, and he thought of me as a friend. Charlie didn't have too many friends.

"He told me about his high-school years," she continued. "He and a bunch of other guys who were into technology called themselves the 'Digital Dukes.' You can imagine how they fit in. They thought it was funny to do things like make jammers and jam the reception on the other kids' Walkman radios, or hack their way into the school system and change people's grades."

"So now you have a free week ahead of you," Lucy said, changing the subject abruptly, and cutting into Karen's private thoughts as she so often did.

"Well, of course, I wouldn't have wanted it this way," Karen replied, catching Lucy's eye. "But I did think I'd take in the new exhibit at the Naples Art Museum...like to go along?"

"It's on me," Lucy said. "Let's go."

Chapter 3

Karen and Lucy drank in the Art Museum exhibit, a flamboyant show of colorful blown glass in monumental arrangements by Dale Chihuly, another Pacific Northwesterner. To lose herself before the towering shapes, full of motion and sparkle, lifted her spirits from the horror of the previous week and the heavy feeling about the one coming up.

The two drove back to Bonita Springs. They decided to pick up lunch at the carry-out counter of the popular Doc's Beach House and enjoy the outdoor picnic tables right on the beach. On weekends during the tourist season, it was hard to get a table, but mid-week they handed Karen's car keys to the parking lot attendant and walked right up to the counter. The restaurant had a second-story bar with tables featuring a view over the Gulf, but Karen wanted fresh air and sand under her feet. It didn't take a long wait to produce their crab salad sandwiches, and they emerged to find a table with an umbrella.

Compatible as the two friends were, they were a contrast to see—Karen was tall with English looks: blue-gray eyes and not-quite-blonde hair and. Lucy was an Irish redhead who loved the sun but couldn't take it in even small doses without hats, umbrellas, and a powerful sunscreen.

"So who's next?" Lucy asked.

"It's an old friend—a next-door neighbor really—from when I lived in New York State," Karen replied. "He and his wife were close friends of Tom (my ex) and me at one time—all four of us—but I haven't seen him for many years, and he's still in Utica. He's a professor at a community college near there. And I'd better not forget to call him *Dr*!"

They paused to watch a pelican swoop into the shallow Gulf water.

"What's bringing him to sunny Bonita Springs in March?

"It's a conference he's going to. Some English teachers' thing. He's going to pocket the money they give him for a hotel and stay with me." Karen pushed her tea aside.

"Have you ever heard of saying 'No'?"

"I just can't think when they're on the phone asking," Karen replied. Her friend had often remarked on her inability to refuse any request from any acquaintance. "I guess deep down I'm afraid to lose some connection to people—no matter who the people are.'

"We've covered this territory before," Lucy answered. "Believe me, you have enough *true* friends. You're not going to wind up watching soap operas and making macramé purses to while away the lonely hours."

Karen laughed. "I suppose you're right, but all my good resolutions just desert me when people are on the phone."

Lucy picked up the wrappers of their lunch and took threw them away. When she returned to the table, she dropped the old subject and returned to Craig. "What does he do for fun?"

Karen sighed. "He thinks he's outdoorsy. I guess I'm going to have to take him hiking to Corkscrew Swamp and Ding Darling Nature Preserve. And maybe kayaking or boating."

Lucy sang to her, "These are a few of my fav-o-rite things!"

Karen laughed. "He's not bringing his wife, Lisa. She works at a day-care center, but they have no kids of their own. I expected her to come along, but I guess she couldn't get away."

"How long do you have till he arrives?"

"He arrives day-after-tomorrow. I'm going to spend tomorrow grocery shopping and washing windows and making up the bed and...you know the drill."

Karen took a last look out at the aquamarine Gulf, scanning the horizon for dolphins. She wished she could find a way to enjoy days like this one more often.

The week sped by far too fast. She was forced to go to the Coroner's office to sign a statement. Dr. Husey wasn't available, so his secretary took care of the paper work. Then there was another afternoon at the Peaceful Rest Home, trying to guess what Michelle would want for her brother's memory, but otherwise, Charlie disappeared from her life like cheese from a mousetrap.

* * * *

Karen often thought of Lucy as a sister. They were so close, they could read each other's thoughts and finish each other's sentences. Lucy had shared with Karen the kind of pain that divorce leaves in every woman—Lucy's husband had simply fallen in love with a co-worker at his insurance company and asked for his freedom. They'd had no children, so it all happened quietly, but she spent years recovering from the rejection.

Singing required Lucy to project a confidence and upbeat smiley charm that didn't come easily at this time in her life, but Karen believed it was the key to her recovery. She relentlessly encouraged her friend to enter every talent contest and amateur show she could find.

Karen wondered what a real sister would be like. An only child, she felt keenly the absence of family. Now divorced, with no children, her parents dead for many years, she was just about completely unattached except for the created family made up of her friends. People she knew who were embroiled in family feuds told her she was lucky.

Her marriage to Tom had begun with hopes for a houseful of children, but each year there was some reason or another to postpone starting their family. On some level, she reasoned later, they knew the marriage wouldn't sustain the addition of parenthood. Tom needed to succeed in the publish-or-perish game that academic teaching requires, and Karen taught English in the town's high school, running more and more school activities. Sex dwindled from frequent to occasional to seldom. Tired from the absorbing work of high-school teaching, Karen went to bed first and feigned sleep when Tom came up the stairs to their bedroom.

When Tom told her they'd be going to Seattle for a year's sabbatical, she was annoyed—there were so many things to take care of: renting out their home, pleading for a leave from her rigid school system, finding someone to take care of their cat Jonah, and talking her colleagues into taking over all her activities. But as always, she did what it took to meet her image of what a wife was supposed to be.

During the year in Seattle, both had time to think about their relationship. It wasn't so much anger at each other—the marriage was simply empty. Even her occasional suspicion of his infidelity failed to rouse passion or anger. Somebody once told Karen that the opposite of love isn't hate, it's indifference, and that rang true to her. There was nothing holding them together, and as the months went by, she dreaded returning to her nosy small town in New York State with its freezing winters and muddy spring thaws. What did she have to look forward to but her retirement banquet when she reached 65? In Seattle she could start over, with a vibrant, exciting, cosmopolitan city to enjoy.

So she suggested that Tom return to New York State alone, while she'd stay on in Seattle. In some ways she hoped he'd object, he'd tell her he loved her so much he'd try to help breathe life into the marriage. But he agreed all too quickly. It seemed to Karen that his pride was hurt more than anything. There was so little love left in their marriage that there wasn't even much of the flare-up of hate that usually follows a decision to divorce. After they made the decision, they continued to live comfortably in their rented apartment until it was time for Tom to leave. Karen drove him to the airport, and they parted with a friendly kiss goodbye. And so her eight-year marriage died "not with a bang but a whimper."

Tom remarried immediately—"as soon as he got a load of dirty wash," Karen always explained. She was hurt but not surprised by the speed at which he replaced her. Perhaps he'd been involved with someone all along.

Meanwhile, she resumed using her own name (her "maiden name") and talked her way into the software business as a technical writer, persuading management that they needed someone like her to translate technical terms into language that normal people could read—and her ploy succeeded. She wound up working at Shangri-la—Microsoft—and eventually partook of the great good fortune of Microsoft's stock options.

Microsoft demanded long hours, so there wasn't much time for dating. She reasoned that she needed a job more than she needed a boyfriend. Microsoft was perfect for a person who deals with personal crisis by avoidance—she had no time left for reflection on where her life was headed.

To complicate life in Seattle, Karen fell victim to seasonal affective disorder—sensitivity to the winter gloom that caused depression. While barely maintaining her professional front, earning promotions and high ratings at her job, she found it harder and harder to get out of bed in the morning, and she spent her evenings watching vacuous television shows. She found herself heading to the vending machines for junk food fixes several times a day. As her size expanded, she thought maybe the term "software giant" really referred to her. She fought against taking the antidepressants that had been prescribed. "Christian women didn't take pills to change their moods,' she told her exasperated doctor. Eventually she realized her job performance was threatened by her condition, so she gave in and started taking medications, but she knew her days of success at Microsoft were numbered.

Meanwhile her stock options mounted steadily as Microsoft declared split after split and the share price rose. While she was preoccupied with her own internal crisis, she found herself one of the fabled "Microsoft millionaires." Her dream of early retirement would come true—and she could find the sunniest place in the country to spend those happy years. Scouting trips to southwest Florida heartened her—when she found her little third-floor condo in Bonita Springs for what she considered a dirt-cheap price, her spirits lifted and she began tapering off the antidepressants.

Retired at such a young age, mending from the depression, slimming down, and enjoying renewed energy, she began to ask questions about her own life. How could she have wound up completely alone? She was good at making friends, of whom she had a large circle, but where were the children, the cousins, the nieces and nephews, the warm extended family that got together for barbecues on the Fourth of July?

She remembered her first cousin Hank (Henry Sinclair). They'd been next-door neighbors, and Karen could remember running after him around the yard their families shared. She tried with all her might to run as fast as Hank, and never, never caught up to him. Her father lost touch with his brother, Hank's father, when the children were in grade school, and she'd been so preoccupied with her own friends, moving far from her parents' home town, she hadn't thought much about her cousin.

Using Internet search tools, she found an address for Hank in New Jersey that might be his. She sent off a letter asking if he was the Henry Sinclair who used to live in Oneida, New York, if he might remember a cousin named Karen, and if he would like to get in touch. She enclosed her phone number and e-mail address and mailed off the letter.

What would Hank be like today? Would they resemble each other? Would he have a family of his own? Second cousins she'd never met? Would he remember her? Would he even reply? Did she even have the same Henry Sinclair…it had to be a common name. Could Hank be the key to the big family she longed to join? She tried to put her musing out of her mind to get organized for the upcoming visit of her old friend Craig.

* * * *

At the end of her precious few days alone, Karen met Craig at the Fort Myers airport. The disheveled scowling man who emerged from the plane had more wrinkles, and less hair, than she remembered.

"Hey, Karen! You're looking good. Retirement agrees with you!"

"You should try it," she replied cheerily. Both of them dived toward the same side for a hug and collided awkwardly. On the second try they got it right.

"No, I love my work, and I've put too much into it to give it up. Still, it's draining to try to bring up the cultural level of a new batch of ignorant freshmen every year. I swear the high schools are teaching them less and less as time goes by."

"I didn't love my work with software as much as you loved teaching. You were the best at being dedicated to your work," Karen recalled.

"Better," Craig said. "Always use the comparative when you're comparing two. Use 'best' only if you're comparing three or more—it's the superlative."

"I'll remember that," Karen answered as Craig dove into the crowd to retrieve the first piece of his Burberry plaid luggage.

On the way home from the airport, Craig blurted out the reason he was traveling alone. "Lisa wants a separation."

"Why? You've been married so long—almost ten years, isn't it?"

"Yes, eight last January, plus two years living together before that, so we'd be sure. I don't understand it at all. I thought there was some other guy, but who—whom— would she meet at a day-care center?"

Karen's thoughts ran to the chubby, motherly woman Craig had chosen. She must have wanted children, maybe met that need for herself by working with toddlers. Karen and Tom had attended their wedding. The Bible reading—the passage from Corinthians about love—had struck Karen forcefully as she realized how far from that ideal her own love for Tom had grown. "I'd sure be surprised if Lisa strayed."

"You mean 'surely.' No, she says—get this—I'm cold and unemotional and she can't tell if I love her."

"Do you love her?" Karen asked.

"Of *course* I do. But I don't go telling her every five minutes, and that seems to be what she wants."

"Speaking as a woman, I can tell you I really like assurances of love. It's important to know you're loved. I can understand. What would be the harm in saying those things once in a while?"

"Speaking as a veteran of a long marriage, it's not the way I want to live. It seems to me two people can go about the business of their lives without wallowing in their emotions every day. It's *sick*."

Karen ignored Craig's misplaced modifier instead of pointing out that he meant "Speaking as a veteran of a long marriage, I don't want to live this way." She remembered her own joyless marriage and felt a pang of sympathy for Lisa. "It's not sick to want to be loved."

"You and Tom divorced and I see you're doing just fine. And Tom has remarried…I see both of you better off for your divorce."

"It's not that simple, Craig," Karen warned. But she hoped an intimate conversation about her own divorce wouldn't be necessary. Karen had disappeared from the picture by staying on in Seattle, and she feared Craig would want more of an explanation than the taciturn Tom had probably given him.

Back at her condo, Karen helped Craig lug the suitcases into the guest room. Why did he have so much luggage? She sniffed cautiously to make sure she was free of the stale odor of Charlie's occupancy.

"O.K. with you if I smoke my pipe?" Craig asked.

"Go ahead." Karen sighed. More smells to purge after Craig's visit. "It would be nice to light up out on the lanai so the smoke would dissipate, and you know my cat is sensitive to it, but make yourself comfortable."

"You still have that old cat?" Craig asked.

"Yes, Junior's 12 now but still frisky!" Karen answered. She knew Junior would hide under the double bed in her room until he was ready to approve Craig, which might not happen at all.

Craig got out his pipe-smoking paraphernalia— tamping tool, pipe cleaners, lighter, pouch of custom-mixed tobacco, heavy on the Latakia, a mix he'd shared with Tom when they were all so close. A shower of tobacco fell from his pocket as he prepared to light up.

Karen opened the refrigerator to get out deli ham, Swiss cheese, bakery rye bread, and Bibb lettuce. She arranged it all on a white platter and started slicing fresh Florida tomatoes with one of her French carving knives. She set the table with a hibiscus she'd picked in the morning and floated in a saucer of water.

"You're still eating meat?" Craig asked.

"Well, I thought you might like a ham sandwich after your flight…"

"I'll just eat the cheese with these tomatoes and lettuce. I hope they're all organic."

"I'm not sure," Karen answered.

"Incredible the levels of poison the Federal government still allows on our vegetables," Craig told her. "You really should shop for the organic vegetables. Costs a little more, but hey, you can afford it, can't you?"

"I'll look for them next time." Karen wondered if his pipe tobacco was organic.

While Craig busied himself unpacking and arranging his things in the guest room, Karen thought about Lucy's teasing. Why couldn't she say "NO" when people invited themselves to visit? If she didn't have a polite social lie at her fingertips ("Oh, darn, that's the week I scheduled my face-lift"), she couldn't say an honest "No."

People who'd lived in Southwest Florida for a long time had a full repertory of put-downs, which they loved to share, laughing and slapping their thighs when they heard a new one. "Oh, you're coming? Well, call me after you get settled into your hotel and we'll have lunch!" for example. "Come again when you can't stay so long!" And you could buy one towel in an exclusive Naples gift shop that said "Don't mistake endurance for hospitality" or another that said, "If we get to drinking and ask you to stay until Tuesday, remember, we don't mean it."

A friend had given her a cartoon with a couple placing a "mosquito farm" under the guest bed. "A helpful hint!" the friend had scribbled across the clipping. And everyone owned the pillow embroidered with "You never know how many friends you have until you buy a house in Florida."

She asked herself where her wimpiness came from. Karen had grown up in a country house far from the suburbs her friends lived in, the ones with no fences and swing sets in the yard. So she spent most of her time with adults, learning their vocabulary and speech patterns.

When she went to school, the other children thought she was peculiar. "Why do you talk funny?" they'd ask. Desperate for their approval, she'd tried to discard her own speech for their childish slang, but she'd been an outsider through all those painful years. Perhaps all that accounted for her need to do whatever other people asked of her. Somehow she'd been able to pass for a crisp, smart, tough-minded professional during working hours at Microsoft, but that had felt like play-acting, and now she was on her own.

She'd read all the books about assertiveness, even taken a class. The participants, all extremely *nice* middle-aged ladies like herself, practiced by sending food back at restaurants or asking for different tables. But when people were on the phone, she forgot all her training. An old friend and her husband had called the previous year. "March isn't a very good month for me," Karen said, thinking this would be a devastating refusal. But the reply was "Oh, we won't be any bother." And they came anyway. Would it ever end?

Craig emerged with camera in hand. Karen had a flashback for a moment. She saw Charlie emerging from the same guest room with his camera in hand, just as they set off for what would be the last day Charlie's life. But Craig's was a still camera, not a camcorder like the one Charlie had used. "Let's go see some of the territory," he said. "The conference starts tomorrow and I'll be busy for a few days."

"Fine," Karen replied. "Let's start out with the Everglades Wonder Gardens. They have a great collection of Florida wildlife." She knew she'd have to go there again if she was to get her life back to normal.

"Isn't that something like a zoo?" Craig asked.

"I suppose so, but the animals were all found in distress, injured or abandoned, so it's not as if they took healthy animals out of their environment," Karen told him.

"Well, we can do that now, but next week, after the conference is over, I want to drive down to the Everglades, see some animals in their natural habitat."

"Fine," she replied, thinking regretfully about the days she'd have to spend as tour guide to the parks she'd seen again and again.

Chapter 4

At the entrance to the Wonder Gardens, the ticket-taker froze when Karen presented the money for their tickets (when it came time to pay, Craig became deeply absorbed in a mounted exhibit of dried molted snake skins on the opposite wall). "Just a minute," the woman said as she slid off her stool and clumped behind the door to the office.

Curly came out and smiled at Karen. "Back again?" he asked. "Bring anybody with you?"

Karen thought for a moment of Charlie pitching headlong into the crocodile pit. She banished the picture that came to mind and asked, "Is that a problem?"

"Of course not. Glad to have you!" Curly answered, just as Craig showed up. Karen made introductions all around. Now that Karen was in a calmer frame of mind, she noticed Curly's deep suntan and blue eyes.

"Know him?" Craig asked as the two entered the park.

"We met last week. It's a long story," Karen told him.

The two turned their attention to the park. Occupying only about a city block, and arranged around a circular path, it was a pleasant walk with the guide. After the tour, guests were free to return to the animals they wanted to see again. The guide took them past the 14 ½-foot captive Florida crocodile, the albino pythons in their cages, and the collection of huge native birds. The path meandered over a rickety suspension bridge that crossed over the alligator pond. The guide fed the alligators as the tourists swayed on the bridge, looking down at the snapping jaws below.

The Wonder Gardens had a large collection of the endangered Florida panthers, breeding them in captivity at a rate faster than their growth in the wild. Tourists saw an injured eagle, an iguana, all of Florida's snakes, venomous and non-venomous, bobcats, and even a few raccoons. The tour ended with Mort the Otter racing a ladder to slide into the water again and again for fish rewards.

Craig turned his attention to Luke and Slewfoot, the Florida black bears who had come to the Wonder Gardens when their mother was killed in a car accident. The charming bears would rear up and eat dog biscuits from the guide's hand so the tourists could see them at their full height.

"Your friend Curly is following us," Craig observed.

"I guess he doesn't want anything to go wrong." Karen turned to Curly and waved. "Everything's fine today!"

The tourists followed the guide on to the panthers. One of the females was in heat, and she was caterwauling so loudly they could hardly hear the guide. Curly was still a few feet behind them. "I think Curly has a thing for you," Craig said. Karen ignored him.

At the crocodile pit, the guide warned the tourists to stay far back from the fence. Karen noted that he was new—she'd been here often enough with guests that she thought she knew them all. She wondered if there had recently been a lot of turnover among tour guides. "If you fell into the crocodile pit, you wouldn't survive," he told the awed tourists. Karen was afraid he was going to use the horrible example of Charlie, but the tourists were a docile lot and kept their distance.

At the end of the tour, Curly escorted them out to their car. "Y'all come on back soon," he said. Karen was pretty sure he didn't mean it.

What's for dinner?" Craig asked Karen as they got in the car. This was Karen's first clue that he wasn't planning on taking her out.

"I'd planned on picking up some Florida grouper and serving it with avocado and tomatoes. It's a recipe most of my guests like," she said.

"Excellent." It was the first suggestion Karen had made that met with Craig's complete approval. They stopped at a small market, and Karen paid for the fish and fresh vegetables while Craig busied himself watching the crowds that lined up at the fish counter, oblivious to her presence until she signaled that she'd finished her transaction there.

Craig ate heartily, as Karen knew he would. She remembered from the days she and Tom had socialized with Craig and Lisa that he loved any garlicky, faintly Mediterranean, type of dish. He went out onto the lanai to smoke his pipe while Karen cleared the table and loaded up the dishwasher. Karen wondered when she could sit peacefully on her lanai again.

* * * *

Fortunately, the next morning Craig had to go off to his conference. After dropping him off at the hotel he was supposed to be staying in, Karen busied herself vacuuming the floors, with a break for the crossword puzzle and some e-mail to Lucy. "Two weeks of Craig is stretching out before me," she wrote, "and I really wish I'd been able to tell him he'd have to stay at his hotel."

Karen thought back to her assertiveness class. She'd rehearsed a speech that went like this: "I won't be able to entertain any more house guests now. I'd love to see you, but I can't have you stay with me." No apologies, no excuses, no lies, just the unvarnished truth. She'd taped it next to the phone and said it to herself like a mantra. "I won't be able to entertain any more house guests now, I won't be able to entertain any more house guests now."

But it all turned to vapor when someone called. Craig had said he wanted to see her, had something to talk to her about. Are all women dupes for the man who needs nurturing and mothering? Then he said he really had money problems and saving on the hotel would help him out of a fix. She remembered the hand-to-mouth existence of a college professor and thought guiltily of her own nest egg from the high-tech business. Surely she could share the bounty she'd been given. So she said, "Fine, Craig, just let me know the details, like when your flight arrives."

"Are you using 'like' as a conjunction?"

So now she was stuck. And it sounded as if he really wanted to go the outdoor route for his visit.

She sat on the sofa and enticed Junior to come sit with her. The cat had been hiding out under her bed and now felt maybe it was safe to emerge. After a moment or two of cuddling, and a few sandy licks to her wrist, Junior began to purr, finally settling into a steady buzz of contentment. If only this could last, Karen thought.

Her little condo was the perfect peaceful haven after her years of fast-paced work in the software world. In those days, home was always an untidy mess with laundry piling up, tea mugs in the sink, and dirty windows. In retirement, Karen kept her tiny three-bedroom apartment home like a little jewel box. It was on the third floor (with an elevator) so her lanai gave her a view of a lake and some wild sanctuary land behind.

Later that night, Karen had to go back to Craig's hotel and bring him to her apartment so he could sleep free in her guest room. And so the next three days passed, with Karen chauffeuring Craig like a soccer mom. His unaccustomed choice of a necktie for the second and third days led her to believe he was interviewing. Could he be preparing to leave Lisa? Was this what he was leading up to in his confession of marital trouble? Were there any colleges near Karen where he might go? Should she be emphasizing the difficulties of living in Florida, working harder to make it seem unappealing?

She remembered the day she arrived from Seattle, muted with Prozac, aching from carpal tunnel, and starved for sunlight. She'd caught a look at herself in the airport mirror, her body swollen with fat from vending-machine food, and her face doughy-white. She'd slouched along toward the baggage claim, scarcely lifting her feet as she walked. Two years in Florida had left her slim, agile, happy, and thankful for every morning. Had she been radiating this change to Craig? Was she inadvertently a walking advertisement for life in Southwest Florida?

Get a grip, she told herself sternly. You're imagining things. Craig has said nothing about actually leaving Lisa. Don't jump to conclusions. Just the same, when she awoke on Craig's first free morning, she prepared to make it clear that Florida isn't for everyone. She would describe the biting ants that left your feet swollen for three days and three sleepless nights; she'd mention the cases of snakebite, so numerous they weren't even mentioned in the papers; and of course, the golfers who'd follow a ball into a water trap and run out with an alligator in pursuit.

She put on a pot of coffee, though she was a tea-drinker and never touched coffee. She was squeezing fresh orange juice when Craig appeared for his breakfast. "What's the agenda for today?" he asked.

"Are you tired from the conference? Would you like to take it easy for one day before we start seeing Florida or—"

"Not at all! You mentioned something about seeing the Everglades. I can't believe we're so close to a national park!"

So after feeding Craig and cleaning up, Karen made sure Craig had everything he needed. Mosquito repellent, sun block #30, hat with a brim ("not that your hair is actually receding or anything, actually we all wear them"), and walking shoes. She didn't have the heart to tell him to wear high boots (against snakebite) in the sweltering sun, but she did veto the sandals.

Shark Valley was an hour and a half away, so Craig had plenty of time to tell Karen more about himself. Of most concern to her was his perception of his marriage troubles. He sounded as if he thought a divorce would be no more bother than moving to a new apartment.

"When Tom and I split up," she told Craig, "we were both in therapy for a year. Neither of us would ever go through that again, even though our marriage wasn't very happy and we're both better off now. You can't imagine how disorienting it is. Everything else in your life goes to pieces for a while. Nothing seems to work right. You can't keep it separate from your life."

"But Lisa wasn't the right choice for me. I can see that now. She's so shallow, maybe because she spends all day with toddlers."

"If I had it to do over, I'd try harder to fix it before taking that last step. I've been there; I know what I'm talking about. I hate to think about you facing what I went through."

"Possessive before a gerund," said Craig.

They arrived just in time for the tram at Shark Valley. Karen lined up to pay for their tickets as Craig headed for the men's room. The guide explained that they'd be riding toward a tower in the middle of the park where they could climb up for a view of the territory. Since the Everglades must be the flattest park in the U.S., and they had a bright, sunny day, they could see for miles around. En route to the tower, they could expect to see alligators, turtles, snakes, herons, and bright white ibises.

"Gator!" shouted one of the children in the seat behind Craig and Karen.

The tram driver stopped and the tourists pulled out cameras and began snapping pictures of the reptile wallowing in the mud, unaware of his sudden celebrity. March was a dry time because the rainy season wouldn't begin until May. The alligators were hard put to find the wet places they loved.

The guide pointed out birds, and plants, and Craig listened attentively, storing up facts to add to his pedantry. She could hear him regaling Lisa with his new information when he returned, while she waited for him to notice her new perfume or the flower arrangement she'd made for the table.

The tram ride stopped at the tower, and Craig and Karen started the gentle circular walk up to the top. Craig was photographing turtles and alligators from above, while occasionally untangling his binoculars from the mass of straps around his neck to look off into the distance. Karen had never seen the view through binoculars, but Craig made no offer of them.

"I could never figure out why you and Tom split up," Craig told her.

"It wasn't a big crisis, nobody finding another love or anything like that, just that we'd grown apart from each other. So when we went to Seattle for his last sabbatical, I thought 'I could live on my own here!' After I suggested it, I regretted it, though, and wished I could have unsaid it."

"Did you try to get back together?" Craig asked as he extricated his pipe-smoking equipment from his camera pouch and started packing the bowl of his pipe.

"We made the occasional attempt at reconciliation— he'd come out to Seattle to see me, but didn't want me back. He took up with Marcia about that time, as you can remember. Tom really hated being alone—I always said he remarried as soon as he had a load of dirty wash, but that wasn't really it—he just liked being married. It didn't matter so much to who. Whom. I was preoccupied with getting a career off the ground, since I was pretty sure I'd be self-supporting from then on.

"Things probably would have been different if we'd had children," Karen went on, entering into territory she rarely spoke about with anyone. "Have you thought of children?"

"God, no!" Craig huffed. "She gets her fill of them at work, and I don't like them."

"I think that's what would have made us a family," Karen said, really speaking to herself now. "We weren't a family, just a couple. I don't think there's a lifetime bond between a couple until children come. I'm only speculating, of course."

Her thoughts drifted back to her marriage. Desperate to be loved, she'd become clingy and dependent—Tom had become more and more distant.

Craig ignored her, pulling out his lighter and starting the ritual of lighting, puffing, and tamping down the tobacco. "If I don't make an effort to win Lisa over, if I decide to let the marriage go, it will be once-and-for-all, final, snap, like the sound of a bone breaking."

"Craig, I know you don't oversimplify things in your research. That's what you're doing here. You're annoyed about a few things Lisa is doing, you're hurt that she brought up the idea of a separation, and you're going to throw over an otherwise good marriage—you'll never find a loving wife like Lisa, nowhere in the world."

"You don't understand," Craig said.

Karen understood better every day. Maybe she'd better let things run their course. Lisa would grieve a while, as she had, but in the long run, everyone would tell her, she'd be better off. And Karen knew that was true too. Even if she never found love in her life again, she wouldn't be looking for it from a source that didn't have it to give. And she wondered if Craig corrected Lisa's grammar every day.

The two spent a few moments looking out over the Everglades from opposite sides of the tower. Alligators and giant turtles basked on rocks in the sun. For a moment Karen envied their lazy lives—lie in the sun, wallow in the water, occasionally gobble up an unwary rodent.

Chapter 5

The next morning Craig woke up with his boundless energy undiminished. Neither he nor Karen mentioned the sunburn he'd acquired across the top of his pate, in spite of the hat Karen had urged on him. "Anyplace we can go out on a boat?" he asked while Karen was cleaning up after their meal of grapefruit and French toast.

"We could go kayaking at Lovers' Key," she suggested, trying to sound enthusiastic.

"Great!" Craig answered, just as she'd been afraid he would.

"It's a state park about ten miles from here, and you rent the kayaks and paddle off to one of the small islands if you like. It's in brackish water, so there are no alligators, and the water's pretty shallow for the most part," Karen told him. "You can see the islands the Calusa Indians built up with mounds of shells."

"I'll take my camera. Can you pack lunch?"

Karen sighed and turned to the refrigerator. "Sure, but I still have sliced ham, so if you want to go meatless, maybe you could stop and buy something at a deli on the way."

"Ham will be fine," said Craig. The prospect of paying for a meal seemed to overcome his vegetarian principles.

Karen leaned down to the bed, reached underneath, and scratched Junior's ears to say goodbye. The cat had been hiding for most of Craig's visit, and Karen felt a pang for her lonely little pet. She whispered a promise to him that they'd spend lots of time curled up on the sofa together after Craig left.

"That old cat can't last much longer," Craig said.

This was too much. "I love the cat, Craig. I love Junior. I hope he lasts the rest of my life. I don't really appreciate you—no your, possessive before a gerund, I know—speculating about his dying," she sputtered.

"I was just stating the obvious," Craig sniffed.

While Karen fumed, Craig retreated into his room. Soon he emerged in an outfit featuring day-glo pink shorts with matching warm-up jacket and sun visor, looking like a cross between Ichabod Crane and a flamingo.

The two rode out to the kayak rental concession in silence. Karen was now counting how many hours before he would leave for New York. It came to 83, including the hour before his flight, when she could drop him off at the airport and go on home, so really it was 82. And then there were the nights when she could sleep, writing off a good seven hours. Maybe she should count only the waking hours she had left. She was lost in her mental calculations until they pulled into the state park.

They looked over the boats available and decided on a two-person kayak, with Karen to paddle up front. They had to carry the boat out to the clear water, their feet squelching deep into the gooey mud at the shoreline. Karen had suggested that Craig take off his socks, but he'd decided to keep them on, so they filled quickly with mud and dragged behind him like a couple of sandbags. Craig's camera and binoculars flapped around his neck and Karen carried the sandwiches, fruit, cookies, sunblock, and water bottles in her day-pack. Finally they lowered themselves into the boat, tipping back and forth as they rinsed off their feet and put their sandals back on.

Karen gave Craig a quick instruction in using the single paddle. Up on the right, lift the paddle, down on the right, lift the paddle, reverse. Craig breezily informed her he'd been kayaking "lots of times." She was surprised at this. Canoes are common in their part of upstate New York, but she hadn't seen many kayaks. He dipped the low side of the paddle so deeply that he hit the sand beneath the shallow water. The paddle began to serve as a brake instead of propelling them forward. Karen wondered if his experience had actually been punting on the Thames or perhaps poling a gondola in Venice.

She turned around and suggested that he dip the paddle a bit more shallowly so they could build up some speed. He returned only an affronted silence, but did adopt a more conventional pattern. He sped up his paddling, as if to outdo Karen, so they lurched forward in a jerky rhythm.

Craig appeared to be strongly left-handed, so his strokes on the left side were more vigorous than those on the right. They began to circle in the water, until Karen suggested he even up the effort on each side. Again he returned only silence, but their progress showed an improvement as he increased the force on the right side.

As they got out into the channel, headed for Mound Key, speedboats passed by them, kicking up huge wakes. Karen had found it was best to head into the wakes, not to let them hit the boat broadside. She suggested this to Craig who told her he already knew about this strategy. Still they missed a couple of times, and the boat grew heavier with the water that had sloshed aboard. "We can overturn the boat and drain it when we stop for lunch," Karen told Craig.

They were heading into the wind, giving their efforts more resistance. Karen hoped their return trip would be easier, with the wind at their backs.

Between the heavy boat and the ragged paddling of the two kayakers, it took nearly two hours to reach Mound Key. They steered along the shore for a while past the mangroves that spread out over the water, until they found a small beach.

"Let's pull in here!" Karen shouted.

At the shore, no topsoil or sand covered the shells that made up the island, so Karen suggested that Craig put on his sandals to pull the boat up on land. He ignored this advice, and soon his feet were streaming rivulets of blood from cuts on both feet. Karen wondered if sharks ever ventured this far into Estero Bay.

"Mound Key was built up by Calusa Indians dumping millions of shells here. If we follow the trail, we'll get to the highest point in Lee County—35 feet," she told him.

He snorted. He reminded her that he was a 46-er, meaning he'd climbed all 46 of the Adirondack mountain peaks with elevations over 4,000 feet. Still, he followed her up the trail to an overlook where they could see the faraway Gulf beaches, the high-rise condos, the boats, and the few uninhabited islands. It was possible to block out the encroaching buildings to get a sense of what it must have looked like to the Indians who lived here so many years ago, before measles and smallpox decimated the tribe.

The two gazed at the vista for a long time, enjoying the silence. Karen finally broke the spell. "How about lunch?"

They settled in on the blanket Karen had carried with her (and protected from the water in the kayak), and took sandwiches, apples, water bottles, and cookies out of Karen's backpack. Fortunately she'd wrapped everything with care so it was dry and still fairly cool.

Craig seemed distracted as he ate his sandwich. "You know, I've been thinking about your life in Florida."

Dear God, no, Karen prayed.

"This would be a great place to make a fresh start. And I've noticed all these new colleges springing up. You know, Florida's the fourth-fastest-growing state in the whole country. Somebody has to teach these kids English," Craig went on.

"Florida's not for everybody," Karen ventured. Her stomach lurched at the thought of Craig invading her sanctuary. She put aside the sandwich she'd just bitten into. "It's really hot in the summer, 92 to 94 every day, and so humid. And some people have a hard time getting used to the bugs—you know we have to use a lot of pesticides. You know, we call our mosquitoes 'swamp angels,' they're that big. And of course, the hurricanes could destroy everything you have."

Breathless, her lunch forgotten, she continued. "Alligators are protected, and they're just everywhere— even in water holes on golf courses. They chase golfers all the time! And during the winter, so many seasonal people come down here from the north, it's like Brooklyn. And with all the construction, the snakes are all coming out of their holes and getting into contact with the people. Just last week I heard about somebody finding a snake in their swimming pool…"

Craig interrupted her. "'His' swimming pool or 'her' swimming pool. The antecedent was singular. Karen, I'd like to live near you when I'm on my own again. I'd like to get to know the person you've become since you left New York. And I know Lisa and I aren't going to make it. I've come to realize that since I've been here." Craig was eating his ham sandwich with great energy, his vegetarianism forgotten.

"You could go back and tell her you understand, tell her you can try to meet her needs, give a little. Marriage is all about compromise," Karen said desperately, offering him her plastic bag of oatmeal cookies.

"Honestly, Karen, one would almost think you didn't want me to move down here!" Craig said with a laugh, helping himself to two cookies.

Almost!

If there ever was a time for the assertiveness training to take hold, this was it.

"Craig, you know, I'm not sure you and I have that much in common except our shared past, and that was with Tom and Lisa. I don't know if you came down here if we'd enjoy each other's company that much," Karen said.

"Let me be the judge of that," Craig said, making Karen absolutely sure she needed to squelch his idea. "You know, I can see you don't have a man in your life."

"I don't think it's a good idea," she said, fighting for sanity.

"Let's talk about it later. You need time to get used to the plan!" Craig said, putting the wrappers from the lunch into Karen's backpack. She stood up and shook out the blanket, shouldering it for the walk back to the kayak. She balanced the blanket with the backpack on the other arm.

She could tell as they walked back that he hadn't a clue of her reaction. He kept blathering about the good feeling he had about Florida. Her throat closed up and she wasn't able to say a word. Surely he must be kidding.

They got into the kayak awkwardly. They were both silent. Karen was afraid Craig saw her protests as some kind of girlish flirtation. How could she make it absolutely clear that if Craig moved anywhere within 100 miles of her, she'd relocate?

They pushed off from the shore, settling into their places, with Karen in the front of the boat, to take up the clumsy paddling pattern they'd established on the trip over. Karen hoped that the current would make the return trip quicker. The silence between them was palpable.

They were only a few feet from shore when a terrific wake came up. Neither had seen the boat that kicked it up—it must have passed while they were struggling to board the kayak. Karen tried paddling hard to turn the kayak perpendicular to the high waves. She didn't want to have to upend the boat again and drain the water that would swamp it if they hit the wave broadside.

As the wave lifted the boat out of the water, she put all her weight into an effort to dip the paddle into the water and take a strong stroke forward, but she spun backwards as her forceful movement met only air. While she was high above the water, pushing with all her might, she lost her balance. The paddle spun out of control and flew out of her hands. It met something solid, and she heard a sickening "crack."

Why Craig had gotten out of the boat she would never know. Her paddle came down hard on his head as he'd bent over the side of the kayak. Maybe he'd been trying to steady the boat against the wake. Maybe he'd forgotten something on shore and was headed to retrieve it. He lay in the knee-deep water, floating face-down. Blood streamed from his head into the water. He was unconscious and taking in the brackish water.

Karen had to get out of the boat to help him to his feet again. She shouted at Craig, she shouted for help, she shouted for anyone. She tried to stand in the wildly rocking kayak, but was knocked to the floor repeatedly by the waves from the wake. The kayak filled with water, and the paddles floated out away from the boat.

After a few more waves—Karen was beyond counting—the wake subsided and she boat stopped rocking, and she was able to slog through the shallow water to Craig's body. She lifted his head, only to watch it loll to one side. "Craig!" she shouted. "Talk to me!"

She felt instant regret that she'd never taken CPR or first aid. She knew from watching movies that rescuers breathed into the victim's mouth to force the water out and air in, but she had no idea how to do this. She tried to bend Craig's head downward towards his waist, hoping he'd vomit or cough. Water and blood streamed off his soaked hair and om his nose and mouth, but he still didn't move or spe .

"Craig!" she sobbed. No response. Nothing. But she'd read about people who could be revived later. If only she could get help! She grasped Craig under his arms and dragged him to shore, leaving him lying prone on the ground with his head turned to the side, in case the water would run out that way. She went back to the kayak and tried to turn it over to empty it. It took two tries before she could shoulder the heavy boat. Life preservers floated around uselessly. Where was the adrenaline that was supposed to kick in at these times? Then she waded out to one of the drifting paddles and returned it to the boat.

She dragged the boat to shore and hauled Craig's absurdly pink-clad body back into it. Trying to be gentle, she nevertheless bumped his head again and again. Where were all the passing boaters, the other kayakers, the Coast Guard, anybody? Now seated in the back of the kayak, she began to paddle with all her strength.

She had no idea how much time passed before she was able to shout to two men fishing from a small boat. Efficiently, they loaded Craig onto their boat and threw out a line to the kayak to tow it behind them. The outboard motor drowned out any questioning as they sped to shore. Karen shivered and sobbed in the front of the boat, gratefully relinquishing the responsibility to find help.

Lee County responds quickly to boating accidents. It took only moments for the EMT truck and the sheriff to arrive at the state park. One of the EMTs went to work on Craig's body, trying to expel the water and kick his respiratory system into action again, while another cleaned his head wound.

Karen tried to explain what happened. "I hit him with the paddle. It was an accident. I didn't see him and I was trying to get us out of a wake."

The sheriff, whose badge read C. Carroll, asked, "Were you drinking or using any kind of drugs?"

"No, of course not!" Karen answered. By now she was hoarse from shouting and her voice came out in a rasp.

"We'll have to take you into the station for testing," the sheriff told her.

"Of course," Karen said. Would they think she had tried to harm Craig? Of course it was an accident! It had nothing to do with the terrible conversation they'd had over lunch. It could have happened to anyone.

"What time did the so-called 'accident' occur?" Carroll asked.

"I—I don't really know. I didn't wear a watch and I wouldn't have thought to check it anyway. We'd just finished lunch at Mound Key, you see, and we were heading back, and a boat must have passed just before we got into the kayak."

"Did you get a description of the boat?" he asked. He pulled a notebook from his shirt pocket and began writing.

"No, I didn't even see it," she told him.

Answering these questions was infuriating Karen. She wanted only to urge the EMTs on to somehow restore Craig's breathing. They loaded Craig's body onto the ambulance and connected him to an IV while placing a plastic oxygen mask over his face. She was not going to be asked to go along. "Where are they taking him?" she asked.

"Lee Memorial Hospital," the sheriff replied. "You can visit him after I talk to you first." The ambulance left with sirens screaming and lights flashing.

She answered a series of questions identifying Craig and telling the story of his visit.

The sheriff asked, "Where's your vehicle?" He pronounced it VEE-hickle. He told her she'd have to get someone to bring her back to pick it up later.

He urged her gently into the back seat of his car and took her to the Estero police station where she was required to submit urine and blood samples. She was photographed, and that made her realize she was drenched with salty water and spattered with mud and something that looked suspiciously like blood. Should she have a lawyer, she wondered. No! Of course not! It was an accident!

The clerk in the sheriff's office asked all the same questions a second time and noted them as she spoke.

Finally she was allowed to leave, but she had to promise not to travel away from Bonita Springs until further notice.

She called Lucy as soon as she was free. She was relieved when Lucy picked up the phone on the second ring. "Please. Come to the Estero police station on Tropicana Road. It's something I can't explain now, but I need help more than I ever have before." She made a stop in the ladies' room and was horrified to see her lank, muddy wet hair stuck to her head, the red eyes, the bedraggled T-shirt. Without making an effort to tidy herself, she waited in the lobby, watching secretaries and clerks walk by. No one spoke to her. Finally she heard Lucy's step into the station.

Karen blurted out the horrible story in the police station lobby. Lucy managed a warm hug in spite of Karen's wet, dirty condition. She took charge, taking Karen by the hand and leading her out to the green Camry Lucy had driven for years. She drove into Fort Myers to the hospital, stopping at what seemed like every red light and driving at slow speeds in the city traffic. Finally she pulled up the driveway to the emergency room, and Karen jumped out.

"Are you family?" the receptionist asked, eyes never leaving the *People* magazine in front of her.

"I'm the only person he knows here in Florida," Karen said. "His family is in New York."

"Wait here. I'll get the doctor." The receptionist walked quickly down the hall, rubber soles squelching against the tile floor.

A few moments later, a young tired-looking doctor in scrubs appeared and sat beside the two women. "I'm sorry," he said. "He'd been without oxygen too long and there was nothing we could do."

"If only I'd done CPR!" Karen wailed. "I didn't know what to do. I could have saved him."

"You mean you didn't even try to clear his breathing passages?"

"I wasn't sure how to do it. I've never had a course or anything. I thought I'd cause more harm."

"CPR doesn't really save people, it just gives them time until you can get them to the hospital. But he might have made it. You can't tell."

Karen would never forget the doctor's words.

It remained for Karen to call Lisa, make arrangements at the Peaceful Rest Home, where she was afraid she was getting to know the staff, and then try to make her life happen again.

"Could you stay a while?" Karen asked Lucy on the drive back to the boat rental concession.

"Of course!" Lucy answered, as if that had been her plan all along.

At the park, Lucy dropped Karen at her car. "Are you OK to drive?" she asked.

Karen wasn't too sure. "As soon as I get behind the wheel, I'll be fine," she answered.

"I'll follow you," Lucy said.

The two drove slowly across the bridge and back to Bonita Springs along the coast. This time Karen didn't mind the elderly drivers in front of her, traveling at 35 miles an hour, with their left turn indicators blinking on pointlessly for miles at a stretch. She listened to a Chopin nocturne on the NPR station and tried not to think about Craig. She remembered the old joke the kids used to tell in high school, "I'll give you a dollar to NOT think about an elephant."

Back in her apartment, Karen took a long shower, applied antibiotic ointment to all her scrapes, washed her hair, put her clothes into the washing machine, and started to clean the kitchen.

"It's not going to get any easier if you keep procrastinating," Lucy told her.

Karen finally picked up the phone and dialed Lisa's number in New York.

"I have some news, Lisa," Karen said tentatively, trying to picture her old friend as she spoke.

"What's up? You and Craig run away together?" Lisa joked.

"Well, not exactly, Lisa," she said, horrified by what Craig had suggested during the last moments of his life. What if she had to call to tell Lisa that she and Craig were going to be together?

"What's it like down there? The snow started to melt here, so all the carrion and dog poop from the winter came to the surface, and then it rained, so it's all covered by a layer of slush and mud. You remember what it's like!"

"That's why I'm long gone!" Karen said, relieved to be talking about weather. "It's beautiful down here, my windows open every night to a tropical breeze and I can still go to the beach in the daytime!"

"So what was it you called to tell me?" Lisa asked.

"It's terrible news, Lisa, and that's why I don't even know where to begin telling you what happened today. Craig's been in accident."

Lucy sat across the kitchen table from her friend as Karen explained the horrible accident. She scribbled a note on an envelope and passed it to Lucy. "TELL ABOUT THE PADDLE."

"And, Lisa, the worst part? The worst part is that I was holding the paddle, the paddle that killed Craig? I mean it was the force of the wave that made me lose control, but I was actually the one holding the paddle that hit him." Lisa was silent, so Karen rattled on. "If only I'd known how to do some first aid, Lisa, maybe I could have saved him." By now she was sobbing into the phone.

After a long silence, Lisa spoke. "Don't blame yourself, Karen. Craig was doing what he loved to do. It was an accident."

"Do you want to come here, Lisa? I know it's hard to make plans now. Maybe you'd better call me back," Karen said, aching to hang up the phone.

"No, I'll talk to the funeral home and make arrangements. Just let them know I'll be calling and give me their number. I think they can send, uh, the body, anywhere in the country. If you'd like to come up here, I'll have a service or something." Lisa seemed remarkably composed.

"Not unless you need me there," Karen said.

"No, don't worry, I can take care of everything," Lisa told her. Karen continued to marvel at Lisa's efficiency, and at the energy in her voice. Where was the breakdown? Where were the sobs, the wails, and the cries?

Sometimes, Karen supposed, problems have a way of solving themselves in ways we would never have anticipated, and maybe Lisa was thinking along the same lines as Karen. Karen wouldn't have to dissuade Craig from moving to Florida, and Lisa wouldn't have to divorce him. They ended the conversation promising to talk again tomorrow. The horrible tragedy was forging a sisterhood between the two women.

Karen called the Peaceful Rest Home to convey Lisa's instructions. They were to cremate Craig's body and ship the ashes to Lisa in New York. "And if you have any questions, call me, Karen Sinclair." She left her number and address.

"Aren't you the same gal who came in last week with the guy from the Wonder Gardens?" the clerk asked. "Don't often see somebody eaten by crocodiles. That made quite a stir around here. Really different from your heart attack or even your gunshot wound."

"Well, yes, but this was a different sort of accident, you see," Karen answered. "It was an accidental drowning. Completely accidental. They were both completely accidental."

"Yes, ma'am," the clerk replied, assuming the somber tone they use in his line of work.

Lucy helped Karen gather up Craig's belongings. She didn't know if Lisa would want his clothing, hadn't thought to ask. She stacked up his political books, his tourist information, his conference papers, his pipe, tamping tools, lighter, and tobacco pouch. Then the two stripped the sheets and quilt from the bed, working on opposite sides, and threw the linens into the washing machine with the towels. They agreed this would be a good time for liberal use of a disinfectant on the walls. They opened the windows in the guest room to air it before sitting down to the tea Lucy made. Lucy had put some of the homemade oatmeal cookies from the canister onto a plate, but Karen remembered the last time she'd seen those cookies and decided this wasn't what she really wanted.

Usually her refrigerator therapy was conducted alone, so ashamed was she of her furtive habit. But this was an emergency. She made one toasted peanut butter sandwich after another, and munched them while Lucy watched in silent astonishment. There were bananas in the fruit bowl on the counter, and they needed to be eaten before they turned brown.

"I think I'll stay over," Lucy said. "I don't have anything tomorrow until rehearsal."

"But the guest bed…it was…he was…"

"I know. I'll be OK," Lucy said. "Fresh linens and I'll be completely comfortable. Then if you wake up and want to talk, you can just snap on the light in the kitchen and I'll come out."

They played a few games of Scrabble to try to tire themselves. Karen got the letters "wrodn" and put the "w" on a triple-word square. They finally turned in early in the morning.

Chapter 6

Karen woke up early, intending to turn over and go back to sleep. Junior was nestled in the crook of her knee as she slept on her side, and she tried to move without dislodging him. Then the memory jolted her from sleep, and she knew she would not go back. She heard distinctly the sound of the paddle cracking on Craig's skull. She wondered how people who killed others in unavoidable traffic accidents went on with their lives. Did they feel responsible for as long as they lived? Did they relive the terrible scene every morning when they woke up? Did they have just a moment's feeling of relief, like the one she felt that Craig wasn't there any more? No! And then an image of Charlie's mangled body came to her mind. Just a couple of weeks ago the biggest problems on her mind had been the appearance of a few gray hairs. Suddenly she wondered if her hair had turned white overnight, like a character in an Edgar Allen Poe story. She jumped out of bed to check the mirror. No, she looked the same as she had yesterday.

She wandered out to the kitchen just as the phone rang. What time was it? Could Lisa be calling again? The police? "What fresh hell is this?" as Dorothy Parker asked.

"Hello," she managed hoarsely.

"Hello, Karen Sinclair? I'm not sure of the number."

"Who's calling?" she asked warily.

"It's Curly."

She searched her memory for Curly. The name was familiar. Just at that moment, Lucy appeared at her side and handed her a mug of tea. That would help. Curly? She knew it was somebody in her life.

"From Everglades Wonder Gardens. Remember?"

"Oh, of course. I wasn't expecting to hear from you." That whole horror came back to her mind. Curly helping her after Charlie's death and then following her around when she brought Craig to the Wonder Gardens.

"I saw the news in the paper," he continued.

"The paper?" Karen asked. She hadn't seen it yet. She looked up at Lucy, who put a copy before her. There was the headline: "KAYAKER DIES."

"Oh God, no, no, no!" Karen gasped, dropping the paper as if it contained a rattlesnake.

"It's obvious this is a hard time for you—I'd just like to take you out to dinner. I didn't say anything about it when your friend Charlie died, but I lost a friend in an accident once, and I could see the same things in your face that I'd felt. I'll tell you about it. You need somebody to talk to," Curly said.

"What's your real name?" Karen asked. Maybe if Curly had a real name she could continue this conversation.

"William David Aubusson, known for the last five years as Curly. I do have a real name. Don't say no. Let me come to get you at 6:00. We'll go someplace close to home, someplace where we can talk. Just dinner. I really want to help."

"Look, Curly, I don't know you, and you must know that under the circumstances—"

"Don't refuse. Things can't get any weirder, can they? It's just for dinner, that's all. I'm coming at 6:00. I know where you live from the story in the paper. I live just across Route 41 from you. If you'd rather, I'll meet you at a restaurant."

"Well, OK, then you come by at 6:00. I need to hang up now and take care of some things here," Karen said, wanting nothing more in life than to get Curly off the phone. He'd had such a firm manner of speaking, she just couldn't refuse.

Karen explained the strange call to Lucy, who reacted just as Karen expected. "What does it take for you to say 'no'?" The last thing you need in your life right now is a date with an alligator handler, for God's sake. He'll probably have turtle chow or otter poop under his fingernails, and boar bristles on his shoulders, and he'll smell like one of the vultures, and all this topped off with an IQ in double digits and an accent from *The Grapes of Wrath*. Call him back and cancel it. I'll do it for you.

"No, I already said I'd go. And you have to admit I could use some diversion."

"I thought maybe shopping."

"Yes, Karen said, "let's do go shopping, but this is evening. I'll come home and have dinner with him. It'll get my mind off everything that's happened.

"You are out of your mind, positively certifiable," Lucy said, but Karen noticed she was smiling.

The two ate a hasty breakfast and dressed in shorts and sandals. They wanted to be out before the phone rang again. Going to a shopping center should make them just about impossible to find, and that was the whole idea. They headed to Sak's Fifth Avenue and modeled the St. John Knits for each other, trying not to roll their eyes and giggle at the $900 price tags. The saleslady ignored them, easily recognizing that these two women were not the idle rich they were pretending to be. Then they dropped into a jeweler's shop and asked to see the diamond-studded tennis bracelets. This time the salesman took them seriously, never leaving them for a moment as they slipped on sample after sample of high-priced bagatelles. Karen wondered if he'd seen her picture in the paper and knew her to be of dubious character, or if he suspected all his customers of light fingers. By the time they stopped for lunch, without so much as a shopping bag to show for their day, they were pleasantly exhausted.

"Thanks for getting me through the morning," Karen said.

"Now I have to wonder about your evening!" Lucy said. "Do you want me to stay over again just in case? I was planning to spend a few days."

"It isn't fair, since I'm going out," Karen replied. But Lucy could tell Karen wasn't being honest, so she said, "Good, I'll stay. Junior and I can watch an old movie."

The two got back to Karen's apartment just in time for her to shower again and change. What does one wear to go out to dinner with an animal park attendant on the day after accidentally killing an old friend? What could she expect from Curly? Would he dress like Ernest Hemingway on safari, or maybe he'd wear torn jeans and a Harley T-shirt with cigarettes stuffed into the sleeves?

She chose a long, shapeless denim jumper, worn over a pink T-shirt. She'd make it clear that this was a casual evening.

Curly showed up right on time, wearing Dockers and a green polo shirt. Karen couldn't help checking the nails (scrupulously clean) and his shoulders (no boar bristles or other detritus) because she knew Lucy would. She introduced her friend to Curly and was pleased that he showed a modicum of social grace.

"I didn't know you'd be staying here. Like to join us for dinner?" he asked. He got a lot of credit for that in Karen's book.

"No, I promised Junior that we'd watch 'Sleepless in Seattle' and I can't disappoint him," Lucy replied.

"Junior? Do you have children?" Curly asked Karen.

"No, he's a cat," Karen laughed. "He's hiding under my desk just to be safe."

Intrigued, Curly got down on the floor in front of the desk and spoke to Junior, man to man. Karen couldn't hear what he said, but Junior actually emerged and presented his back to be rubbed. Curly obliged and before long the cat turned into a purring rag doll while Curly stroked his fur.

"That's just unbelievable," Karen told him. "Junior takes a long time to make friends."

"I'm used to animals," Curly said. "Let's go. See you later, Junior and Lucy." He turned a smile on Lucy and Karen thought she saw her melt just a little.

It was a long time since Karen had had one of her rare dates. After her divorce, she'd gone to work at a job that took all her energy. She'd had to learn to do work she'd never been trained for, staying in her cubicle office late in the evenings and sometimes whole weekends. Maybe that was also avoidance—after a failed marriage, he wasn't sure she wanted to try again. Besides, the high-tech world was such a young world. The men she met were 15 years her junior—being so close to forty made her a senior citizen. They were amused by listening to rock groups she'd never heard of, playing video games she never got the hang of, or seeing movies featuring space aliens.

"This has been the worst month of your life!" Curly observed as he opened the door for her to get into his green Toyota Corolla. He didn't open it all the way, so they were face to face as she turned to get into the car. Being so close to him startled her and she paused for a moment. He was a bit taller than she, which she appreciated since she'd always been self-conscious about her own height. He was tanned in a way that emphasized the blue of his eyes as he looked into her eyes and beyond. He was developing the small wrinkles and smile lines that people who spent time in the sun always did. It suited him.

Karen recovered herself while Craig walked around to his side of the car. "That pretty well sums it up," Karen answered as he slid easily into the driver's seat. "It seems that it's fatal for anybody to come stay with me."

"Well, the day you brought what's-his-name, Craig? to the Wonder Gardens, I almost pushed him into the crocodile pond myself. I heard him correcting your English. How are you holding up?" he asked.

"Lucy is a big help. She's been there both times when I needed a friend. Beyond that, I'm never really sure how I'm going to get through the next day."

"Where's your family?" Curly asked.

"I don't have one. Only child, divorced, no kids of my own, parents dead...I'm trying to find a first cousin, Hank Sinclair, who might be living in New Jersey somewhere, but we've lost touch since we were kids. I'm not even sure he's still alive—he'd be about 50 today. You can track people down on the Internet and I think I might have a lead to his address. I have no idea what he's done with his life—he might have spent it in the penitentiary."

"No family at all? That's amazing! I suppose people tell you you're not missing a thing. Just the chance for life-long resentment from the ones you love." Curly said as he turned the car into the parking lot of Karen's favorite Italian restaurant.

They ordered a glass of wine while they waited for dinner.

"When I was a teenager, I lived in Germany," Curly said. "I was an Army brat—my dad was stationed in Frankfurt. I had two friends I used to go kayaking with—we were daredevils, the way kids are. Once we took the kayaks out toward one of the locks in the Main river where the water plunged a few feet. There were signs up saying no boating past this point and blah blah, in German and English, but we didn't care. They looked back at me and headed over it. Without thinking, I followed. I don't know how I survived, but both of them drowned. We knew better, I was a year older than they were, and I should have said no, but it was all very fast, and over we went. They were just finishing junior year. I could have stopped them—that's the worst part."

Karen shuddered. At least she hadn't seen Craig's face when the paddle hit him. Had he seen it coming? Did he die instantly? "That's a terrible memory to carry around with you. The worst part is knowing you could have done something. I should have told Charlie not to climb up the fence at the Wonder Gardens—he seemed to be up there before I got a grip—and Craig—I'm the one who hit him—even though it was an accident. I feel as if I'm to blame for both of them. I didn't even want either one of them to come to Florida."

"Freeloader syndrome? It's what happens to everybody in the first few years after you move here. You get more houseguests than you ever dreamed of—people you don't even know that well. Even single men who don't cook have the problem. Pretty soon you learn to say no so you can stay sane."

"I've been trying to learn to do that!" Karen laughed. "It's not as easy as it sounds! I read the book on *Boundaries* and I make serious speeches to Junior, but…"

The waiter brought their antipasto and they started helping themselves to provolone and pepperoncini and salad. Curly picked up a marinated mushroom and dropped it onto Karen's plate. "These are delicious. Try one," he said.

"What's it like working at the Wonder Gardens?" Karen asked.

"I've only been there two years," Curly told her. "I was a biology research scientist for a drug company in the Research Triangle in North Carolina for twelve years. I couldn't stand what we were doing to the animals and I threw it over—pension, stock options, health insurance, and fat salary. The marriage went along with it all. I

71

came down here to run away, and I've been happy working at the Wonder Gardens for hourly money. Nobody understands it at all."

Karen thought of the instant rapport Curly had made with Junior. "You're good with animals," she said.

"Yes, I am. The last day I worked, we were dripping chemicals into the eyes of rabbits. I couldn't watch it any more. I can't think of any scientific advance that justified that. I'll never get it out of my mind. From now on, I'll do what I can for them—like atoning. The Wonder Gardens takes only injured animals from the wild—it's not like a zoo—and I support that."

They paused while the waiter replaced their antipasto dishes with the entrees they'd ordered. Curly seemed to be watching for Karen's reaction to his story. Or watching for something. She couldn't return the intensity of his look, and she found herself squirming awkwardly, so she turned her attention to her pasta.

"I admire you for that," she ventured. "I left corporate life—Microsoft—just because I was sick of the frantic pace to make something I didn't care about. And I left because I could, of course. I never had to do anything there that gave me the kind of pain you're talking about, but all those stock options have a powerful pull. They call them 'golden handcuffs.' It's hard to walk away from them."

As they started to taste their entrees, Karen thought about what it would be like to go to the Wonder Gardens and do hard day labor in the heat every day after he'd been used to a comfortable air-conditioned office where he wore a white coat and where secretaries flirted with him.

"So who's the next visitor at your B&B?" Curly asked.

"Nobody on the horizon," Karen told him. I think I have some free time for a while, and I'll need it with the investigation that's going on into Craig's death. It's hard to explain, but I'm frightened even though it was an accident. I've never even spoken to a sheriff before, let alone been driven to a police station in a police car. I feel guilty just because I was there."

"I'm glad to hear you have some free time coming up," Curly said. "I'd like to spend some of it with you." He took her hand across the table and covered it with his own. She wondered what her heart was doing.

* * * *

"Alligator handler, HAH!" Karen told Lucy triumphantly later that night, as the two of them sat in the living room of her apartment. She filled Lucy in on the surprising story of Curly's past.

"He's intelligent and articulate—he even talks like me!" Karen told her friend. "You know what they say, we could finish each other's sentences."

"Who would have dreamed?" Lucy said, helping herself to the popcorn she'd been working on during her evening alone.

"And he wants to see me again. We're going to the Philharmonic next Saturday, he has season tickets, so how's that for a guy who wears a green shirt with his name embroidered on the pocket?"

"The Philharmonic? Are you sure he didn't say the Motocross races or the Greyhound track?" Lucy asked.

Karen threw a handful of popcorn kernels at her and headed for her bedroom. For once, she would sleep soundly. She wasn't even hungry, although there was plenty of popcorn left in Lucy's bowl.

Chapter 7

Breakfast the next morning was interrupted by the phone call Karen had been dreading. She would have to go back to the courthouse in Estero and answer questions about Craig's death.

Lucy offered to go along, to Karen's immense relief. Lucy borrowed one of Karen's suits and the two dressed somberly. "Let's make a good impression—this is no time to look like bag ladies," Lucy said.

High heels clacking on the marble floors of the courthouse, they found their way to the coroner's office. The secretary left them in uncomfortable plastic chairs with outdated copies of golfing magazines to read while she announced their arrival in the coroner's inner sanctum.

"He's ready to see you," she told them, almost immediately.

Both women headed into the office. "Who's Karen Sinclair?" the secretary asked.

"I am, but I've asked my friend to accompany me," she replied.

The secretary disappeared into the inner office again and returned.

"The coroner wants to know if the friend was present when the deceased was killed," the secretary asked.

"Just afterwards," Karen replied, stretching a point. She knew she couldn't face this alone.

The secretary hesitated. "OK, go on in," she said.

The coroner came toward the door to greet them. "Dr. William Husey, ma'am, Lee County Coroner. I believe we met under unpleasant circumstances at the Everglades Wonder Gardens. Come on in. I have a few questions for you." Although he was only a couple of inches shorter than she, Karen had the feeling that he came up to her shoulder—could those soft-soled shoes have some kind of lifts in them? He seemed to bounce when he walked. He had combed his thin gray hair into a network over his bald spot.

The women followed them into his office. Although some decorator had filled the shelves with leather-bound books and silk plants, piles of papers and files draped over the books ruined the look. Karen noticed a set of hand weights on his desk.

"An object like a kayak paddle was the instrument that caused the death of one Craig Walters," the coroner said, glancing at a file in front of him."

"Yes, he was killed in a boating accident—we were swept up in a boat wake and—"

"I've already decided to rule this death accidental," Husey interrupted. "But I just want to get this straight. You might say I'm just curious."

Karen hardly knew whether to believe his reassurances that he had already made a decision about the case. She was afraid it might be some kind of trap.

"Craig was an inexperienced kayaker. I suppose I am too. We were just launching our kayak when the boat came along at a high speed and kicked up a wake—we were out of control."

"If you were such inexperienced kayakers, why did you go out alone?" Husey asked.

"Craig wanted to see it—and I went along. He—well, both he and I, maybe exaggerated our skill and underestimated the danger."

Husey leaned back in the chair, placed his hands together in a steeple and looked at the ceiling. Was he sitting on a phone book, Karen wondered?

"Usually in a death like this there's some kind of alcohol or drugs. But the tests for both of you came up clean."

"I admit our judgment wasn't very good," Karen huffed, "but we weren't drinking. Both Craig and I drink very little and, well, certainly we wouldn't take that chance when we're on the water."

Husey sat forward and looked intently at Karen. "It says in the next-of-kin that Craig was a married man. Just why was he visiting you?"

Lucy stirred in her chair. Before she could raise an objection to his insinuation, Karen said, "Both Craig and his wife are old friends of mine. He was here on a business trip. I've phoned his wife Lisa in New York State and I'd be glad to have you phone her too if you have any questions about our relationship."

He looked disappointed, but dropped his gaze from Karen and looked down at his report again. Karen wished she could see it.

He continued. "Walters sustained massive head wounds. The skull was actually fractured. I don't know if he could have survived that—or what kind of person he would have been if he had—if he hadn't actually drowned. That's a hell of a head wound for a little gal like you to make."

Karen wondered where *he* got the idea to call *her* "little." She said," The kayak was being slammed down by the force of the wake. If I'd *tried* to hit Craig, I couldn't have done it with that much force by myself alone." She thought back to her last conversation with Craig and the horror she felt at the idea of having him move to Florida. But only she and Lucy knew that conversation had taken place, and there was no reason to tell it to the coroner.

"Well, the immediate cause of death was drowning, that's what's on the report. That's all the questions I have," the coroner told her. "Unless you have anything to add?"

"No, I think you understand how it happened," Karen said. She and Lucy rose and left as fast as they could, exchanging the briefest of handshakes and hypocritical "thank yous" with the diminutive doctor.

They made their way out of the courthouse in silence, as if they might be overheard while on the premises. When they reached Lucy's car, they burst into laughter.

"Were those elevator shoes?" Lucy asked?

"I thought so too," Karen answered between fits of giggles.

"'A little gal like you?' I can't believe it!" Lucy said, wiping her eyes.

"Drinking?!" Karen sputtered. "Let's go have one right now!"

Lucy headed out of the parking lot and back toward Bonita Springs to their beach club, where she knew they could order a drink in mid-afternoon, no questions asked.

Looking out over the beach, Lucy proposed a toast. "To all deaths being ruled accidental!"

"I don't know why it all seemed so funny. Relief, I guess," Karen speculated, removing the umbrella from her daiquiri. "I wondered what would have happened if I'd told that little pipsqueak that Craig was about to leave his wife and come down here to pester me, and that I brained him with a paddle not five minutes later."

"Nobody needs to know that but me," Lucy said, suddenly very solemn.

"You're right," Karen added. "No need to stir up anything suspicious, and Lisa doesn't need to hear that either. Unless he told her about his plans before he left. And I had the impression I was the first lucky person to know."

So Lucy wouldn't have to drive right away, the two stayed on at the club for a long lunch, watching the pelicans fly over the Gulf while they ate shrimp cocktails and Greek salads. "I think I'm going to make it," Karen finally said.

"I've been waiting to be sure of that," Lucy told her. "I think I'll move back home."

* * * *

As soon as Karen bid Lucy goodbye, with promises to call regularly, Karen headed out to the communal mail center to check her mail, which she had allowed to pile up for the last few days. Among the magazines and catalogs and offers of pre-approved credit cards was a hand-addressed envelope postmarked from New Jersey. Karen turned it over to find it was from one H. Sinclair.

She tore into it before she got back to her apartment. "I was glad to hear from you," the letter began. "I am the Hank Sinclair your looking for, and I would like to see you again. My wife Sue Ann and I can come to visit you and get aquainted again. Please call me at 209-566-9313 to talk. It sure is good to find you."

What would Craig make of all Hank's English errors! He'd return it to Hank with "you're" and "acquainted" spelled correctly! She raced upstairs to dial the number. "Hank!" she said when a man answered. She was surprised that he was free to answer the phone at 3:00 in the afternoon, but she had been too excited to think about timing her call.

"Yes, this is Hank Sinclair. Who's calling?"

"This is Karen!" she told him.

Junior, on the sofa halfway across the room, jumped up when he heard the exuberant whoop Hank made into the phone. As only cats can do, Junior made an irrevocable decision that he was not going to like Hank Sinclair. "This is great! Honey, it's Karen!" he shouted, as if to someone else in the room. "Hey, we got to get together again, and soon!"

Another visitor. But this would be different; this one was family. Karen would have a family again. "Sure thing. When can you come down?" she asked.

"We can get right on the road, can't we, honey? Just the two of us, my two boys are grown and moved away. You see, I just got laid off at the chemical plant, and you might say I got plenty of free time till my unemployment runs out. So this is a good time for us!"

"You don't need to go job-hunting?" Karen asked him.

"Something'll turn up when I need it! It won't hurt to take a little vacation till then, hey, Karen? What d'ya think, honey?" he asked.

"Well, that would be great! When do you think you might arrive?"

"We'll be a couple days on the road, first I have to get tires for the truck, and pack up a few things. How about next Friday?"

"Fine, that's great!" Karen told him. You have to exit from Route 75 at Exit 18…"

"Never mind, I got a real good sense of direction, you know? I'll call you when we get closer. I got a cell phone," Hank told her.

After hanging up, she began the familiar routine of making up the guest room and starting a grocery list. The B&B is back in business, she told herself. But this would be different. This would be her family.

* * * *

The next morning's paper carried the headline "KAYAKING DEATH RULED ACCIDENTAL" but it was at least on page two, not right up front in the lead position of page one, and there was no photograph. Karen was sitting down to read it with her tea. Junior, certain that he was more interesting, jockeyed for lap space with the thin local paper. Just as the two settled into a compromise, the phone rang.

"This is Curly," he said, "I read my morning paper before work, and I'll bet you're doing the same thing now."

"Yes, I went to see the coroner yesterday, and I forgot that this would be the likely outcome," Karen answered. Junior purred and rubbed his chin against the phone.

"How do you feel?" Curly asked. Karen could hear cawing in the background.

"It's hard to explain," she answered. "There's no question that I had no intention to harm Craig, but it is true that I disliked him. I mean, I didn't want to see him dead, but I did want him gone. So I feel guilty for no *real* reason. This kind of guilt eats at you."

"You have no reason to feel real guilt about this. I'm off work at 4:00—blue-collar hours—I'll change and get there by 6:00. I'd just like to see you again. We can talk about this if you want and put it behind us."

"Sure. That would be fine." Karen was surprised to hear him refer to "us." There was no "us," was there? What would happen if Karen fell into the languid comfort of another romance? She'd so often dreamed of love, but then given herself the stern lecture about how they always end badly and being alone is really preferable.

She spent a leisurely morning puttering around the guest room and going through an old family scrapbook that held pictures of her with Hank when they were children. They were playing in the back yard they shared, with their mothers looking on. It was summer, a season much appreciated in upstate New York. They had no fancy toys in evidence, but seemed to be having a lot of fun jumping off old packing crates and running around clotheslines. Hank's part-collie dog Scruffy was chasing them in some of the snapshots. It looked like a wholesome childhood, if you didn't know about Hank's father, John Sinclair.

John drank himself to an early death, and she knew her father had given up on him years before. The last call came when he'd been arrested at Syracuse Airport for public drunkenness and needed help getting home.

The family loved to tell the story of one of the nights John was picked up for drunk driving. In their small upstate New York town in those days, arrestees were taken home and told to come in and face the music later. The next morning, when his hangover cleared, John began to feel unjustly accused. He decided to fight city hall. But when he went in to challenge his arrest, he heard the policeman tell the story of how he'd fallen to the ground when they opened the door on the driver's side. He just slumped down into the street. They'd had to take him home in the patrol car.

Karen hoped Hank hadn't gone the way of his father. She'd learned that alcoholism is genetic and she wondered just how it might reappear somewhere in their small family line.

* * * *

Curly was punctual, ringing the doorbell at just 6:00. "It's open," Karen called out.

Curly let himself in and stopped for Junior first. The cat rubbed shamelessly against Curly's pantleg.

"Junior, you are one happy cat!"

"He likes you," Karen said. "I'm a keen observer of the obvious."

"How about you?" Curly asked.

"Me?"

"You could learn something from Junior about greetings," he said, moving toward her and giving her a hug. She liked the fact that she could look up at him. Few of the men in her life had been that much taller than she was. She felt quite at home.

She laughed. "I'm too inhibited!"

"We'll have to work on that. And now we have time. No visitors, just time for each other."

"Well, there is this one interruption," she began, moving out of his embrace and avoiding the real question that was forming between them. "I think I told you I don't have a family, but I do have this one first cousin. I think I mentioned using the Internet to try to locate him. He got my letter and he's coming to see me right away! He could arrive at any time. Look, I have a picture of us from when we were kids."

"So the flower arrangement wasn't for me?" Curly asked, pointing to a vase of chrysanthemums Karen had placed on the coffee table.

"Well, it's partly for you!" she lied.

"I had a great time Sunday night. We're not young— we have to recognize when this happens and go for it. We don't have world enough and time to dance around it. Let's go for a walk on the beach and then have dinner someplace with a view. We can talk and hold hands and maybe I'll find out who you really are."

That sounded good to Karen. Wouldn't it be easy to sink into the arms of this strong man, and start over?

Nature got into the act by providing one of Florida's most spectacular sunsets as they walked along the shoreline. They drove to a restaurant she'd never been to and sat at the window—how had Curly arranged that during the busy season?

As they were sipping their wine, they enjoyed the afterglow of the sunset. They both watched carefully for the fabled "green flash" that's occasionally seen at the moment the sun dips into the sea. Karen had never believed in it, thinking the braggarts who spoke of it were motivated by wishful thinking. But there it was, short but spectacular, as a moment of intense light.

As promised, Curly sat across the table from her and reached for her hand. Their dinner and their bottle of wine disappeared somehow and then suddenly neither one wanted dessert or coffee.

Curly opened the door of his car for her. As she stepped past him, he turned her toward him and kissed her. She gave in to it, leaning against him and letting him set off the chain reaction of feelings she had forgotten a woman could have. Was this reckless? Did she not know him well enough? She didn't care.

He released her reluctantly and walked around to the driver's side of the car. Somehow he freed a hand to take hers during the short ride to her apartment. They walked silently toward her door, not needing to talk to confirm what they both knew they wanted.

But as they rounded a corner, a huge figure bounded toward them from the curb where he'd been sitting under the light. "Karen?" he shouted. As they drew nearer, they saw a man extending his arms for a hug, almost running toward them. "I'm Hank!"

Karen and Curly were speechless. After a long pause, Karen recovered enough to say, "Well. Welcome, Hank. This is my friend Curly. Curly, my cousin Hank, I mentioned him."

A small woman emerged from the pickup parked in the next space. "And I'm Sue Ann! I'm so glad to meet you!" She put out a hand to shake and, still stunned, Karen and Curly reciprocated in turn. Karen tried to catch Curly's eye, but Hank was pumping his hand and telling him about the drive from New Jersey.

"Didn't spend nothing on motels, Sue Ann and me, we just drove on through," he was saying.

They were interrupted by a series of menacing barks from the pickup truck.

"That's Kaiser," Hank explained.

"You brought a DOG?" Karen asked in horror. I didn't know you were going to bring a dog. I have a cat who's not young any more and he'll be frightened. You'll have to keep Kaiser in your room, away from Junior."

"Kaiser won't like that, but hey, he's very well trained. Don't worry about a thing. Give me a hand with these bags?" Hank asked.

Sue Ann went back to the pickup and snapped a leash around the neck of a large black dog, possibly a bit of Newfoundland and a bit of Labrador and a bit of prehistoric mastodon. Karen estimated the dog's weight at slightly more than hers.

"Sure," Curly answered. "But Karen's right about Junior—we need to make sure Junior has a chance to hide before you bring a big dog in there." Kaiser began sniffing at Curly.

* * * *

Everyone shouldered a bag—how long were they planning to stay, Karen wondered—and headed for the apartment. Curly went in first and picked up the trusting cat from the sofa. He put Junior in Karen's bedroom and shut the door. Karen showed Hank and Sue Ann the guest room. While Sue Ann put down the heavy bag she'd been carrying, Kaiser broke free of her grasp and bounded around the living room, knocking over the flower arrangement on the coffee table.

"I'll get paper towels," Karen said. "The guest room is on your right."

While she mopped up the mess from the spilled flowers, Kaiser sniffed her and attempted to mount her kneeling form. "Hank! Get the dog," she shouted.

"Cut that out, Kaiser," Hank said, laughing as he disengaged Kaiser from his cousin. "He's all boy, that Kaiser! The vet told us we ought to neuter him, but I couldn't do that to a dog of mine, know what I mean?" he said, winking at Curly.

"How about a drink?" Karen asked. We can sit down and then we'll have a chance to get acquainted. Here, take the sofa. I know you must be tired from your trip."

"Boy, am I ever," Sue Ann said. In the better light of her apartment, Karen could see the dark circles under the older woman's eyes. "And I need a shower right after that drink."

"You have your own bath right next to the bedroom," Karen said. "What'll it be? Beer? Wine? Cokes? Scotch?"

"I could use a beer!" Hank shouted from the guest room."

"Me too" Sue Ann said.

"We'll go get the drinks," Curly said, steering Karen toward the kitchen.

* * * *

In the kitchen, Curly backed Karen up against the refrigerator, preventing her from opening it and dealing with her guests' requests. He smashed a fist against the freezer door. "Listen, Karen," he whispered. "Whatever hopes I had for tonight are dashed—some day we'll laugh about this. But that dog is bad news. He worries me. Why did you let Hank bring him in here?"

"I didn't know what to say," she answered *sotto voce*, looking up at him. "I couldn't think of a thing. What could I do?"

"How about 'I can't have that dog in my apartment'? You're not very good with 'no,' are you?"

"I'll keep Junior safe in my bedroom," Karen said. "He won't like it, but he'll be safe."

"I hope so," Curly said, releasing her.

She opened the door and pulled out two cans of beer. "Want one?" she asked Curly.

"No, I think I'll head home and let you talk to your cousins," he replied.

As she opened the cans and poured the drinks into mugs, Curly headed out to the living room. "I'll be going now. Have a good visit. Watch that dog, OK?" Curly said as he reached the door.

"Thank you, Curly, for dinner, and…" Karen said.

"Good night," he interrupted, leaving the apartment and closing the door firmly.

Chapter 8

"Nice setup you've got here!" Hank said after a hefty swig of his beer.

"Thanks. I'm happy here. I love Florida," Karen told him, trying not to think about Curly's tone of voice as he left. "How did you find me?"

"You're in the phone book, so Sue Ann asked a guy at the Mobil station. You weren't home when we called—out with Curly, huh? He's your boyfriend?"

"Actually, we've only been out together a couple of times. We're just getting to know each other," Karen told him, praying he'd stop asking her about him.

"So you're divorced from your husband, Tom, right? I heard from my Dad that you'd married some years ago, but we never met him. It's been too long!" Hank said.

"Yes, we've got a lot of catching up to do after all these years!" she said. "Tom and I were married for eight years—no children—and we separated in Seattle. I've been on my own since then.

"Well, I got laid off, you know. It was, like, take this job and shove it, you know. I don't care about the job. Hell, I'll find another one when I need it. There's plenty of factories in Jersey, that's why I put up with the place." Hank laughed. Karen noticed as he lowered his feet to the coffee table, brushing against the chrysanthemums carelessly.

They both downed their beers. "Well, you're probably tired from your trip. I keep the beds made up in the guest room, and there're towels in the linen closet for you…" she said, hoping they'd go to bed so she could think over what to do next. Sue Ann picked up the hint and rose from the sofa.

"Yeah, it's been a long drive. Tomorrow we want to start seeing something of Florida, maybe go to the beach, drive around, you know, take in the sights," Hank said, swatting Sue Ann playfully on the bottom. "Honey, you better take Kaiser for a walk before bed!" She hesitated just a second before smiling and leashed the powerful dog.

When Sue Ann returned from her very short walk, Karen noted gratefully that they took Kaiser with them to the bedroom. She went to her own room and found Junior under the bed. Later, toward morning, she saw that he'd resumed his usual sleeping place on her bed at her feet.

The next morning Karen showered and dressed before opening the door to the bedroom to go out and face her guests in the light of day. Hank was on the lanai, smoking a cigarette, while Sue Ann had fetched the paper and was reading it in the living room. She looked up to say, "I told him he had to go outside to smoke. I can't stand to be around it either. I knew you wouldn't want him smoking in your place."

"Thanks," Karen answered. "Coffee? Breakfast?"

"Coffee, yes, but I don't eat breakfast," Hank announced from the lanai.

Karen went on to toast bagels for Sue Ann and herself, and they joined Hank with their plates and coffee mugs. She didn't bother to fix tea, which she preferred. "How would you like to relax on the beach today?" Karen asked.

"Just the ticket after our trip," Hank said, without asking Sue Ann for an opinion. Let's see if we can find my stuff." He and Sue Ann disappeared into the bedroom.

They emerged shortly, carrying large bags, with Kaiser on a leash. "Ready?" Hank asked.

"Just a minute," Karen said, sweeping up the last of the breakfast. "I need to get dressed. There's a beach in Éstero where we can bring dogs."

"That's great!" Hank boomed. It didn't take Karen long to join them, and they packed beach chairs and an umbrella into the cousins' truck. Kaiser paced around in the truck bed behind them.

Karen directed Hank to what the local people called the "doggy beach," where dogs were welcome to run free in and out of the water. Karen hoped Kaiser would be able to run off some of his energy. She was gratified that he chased sticks inexhaustibly, and raced in huge circles around their beach chairs, for hours. Hank was completely absorbed in his dog's antics.

"So why did you and Tom split up?" Sue Ann asked Karen when Hank was out of earshot. "How did you get along after?"

"I guess we just grew apart, you might say," Karen told her. "Tom remarried right away so he might have had somebody on the side. I don't know, but we just didn't have any spark left in the marriage. When we went to Seattle, supposedly just for a year, I thought I could live independently there, so I stayed on. It was hard getting started again, but now I'm retired and have all my freedom. I found it's just amazing what a woman can do when she has to."

Sue Ann seemed very interested, as if she wanted to ask more questions, but she stopped abruptly when Hank returned. Kaiser shook seawater all over them.

"Kaiser was drinking seawater! How about that dumb dog?" Hank gave Kaiser a signal to jump up and place his forepaws on his chest. Kaiser complied and Hank waltzed around the beach with him for a moment.

"Sue Ann, I think you're getting a sunburn!" Karen told her. "Maybe we'd better call it a day."

"I don't care about that ozone layer stuff," Hank interrupted. "I think a little sun is good for you."

"Just the same, I think I've had enough," Karen said. "Let's go home and change. Maybe we can find a nice place for dinner. What kind of food do you like?"

"Italian," Hank replied, pronouncing it "eye-talian." Sue Ann didn't contribute an answer.

"We've got lots of nice places, then," Karen said.

They drove home in the pickup, with Kaiser sleeping in the bed of the truck. Karen hoped he was as tired as he looked.

Hank read out the signs as he drove. "Wendy's," he announced. "Paper towels $1.49 for three rolls at Walgreen's." Sue Ann ignored him.

Back at the apartment, Karen looked in on Junior, tightly secured in the bedroom, and Hank took Kaiser to the bathroom and took several towels from the linen closet to wipe the seawater off him. The dog emerged and shook himself all over Sue Ann, who was waiting for her turn in the bathroom. But then he turned astonished eyes toward Karen as he vomited copious amounts of seawater all over the eggshell-colored carpet. "Hank!" Sue Ann screamed.

Hank ran to the living room, wearing only his boxer shorts. "Dumb dog! I told you not to drink in the ocean! Sue Ann, go get some paper towels. Cut it out, Kaiser!" He surveyed the spreading puddle and tugged on the dog's collar. "Hey, you drank a hell of a lot of that stuff—there's whitecaps in that thing!"

95

Karen got an old towel from the lanai and the two set about wiping up the mess. Hank took a chastised Kaiser back to the bedroom. Karen sprinkled carpet cleaner over the large spot, hoping the stuff would be effective. The largest challenge it had previously faced was a cat furball.

Finally—dog in guest room, cat in Karen's room, carpet drying, adults cleaned up and ready for an evening out—the three locked the apartment door behind them and headed for the Italian restaurant, Nonna Maria, in Karen's car. "I hope you like this place. It's a favorite of mine."

Hank, seated up front, read "Radio Shack. Gold's Gym. Taco Bell. Hey, look, Sue Ann, honey, they got a Wal-Mart."

They had a wait for a table at the popular restaurant, so they sipped a glass of wine at an outdoor table. Karen was enjoying the first peaceful moment of the day. She wondered what Curly was doing. The waiter summoned them inside and presented them with menus.

"I love scampi!" Sue Ann said. "I think I'll order it because Hank doesn't care for it so we never have shrimp at home."

"That's right—I like meat," Hank announced. "I'll go for the spaghetti and meatballs. You think they got garlic bread?"

"They serve foccacia, a kind of herb flatbread. You dip it in olive oil," Karen explained, assuming that this was probably not in Hank's gustatory experience. "Try it!"

Hank poured a generous amount of oil onto his plate and began wiping it up with the bread. The waitress was quick with their order. Karen tried to keep up with their pace as they ate—still, they had a wait before she finished. No one moved when the waiter brought the bill, so Karen finally reached for it. She thought that since Hank had been laid off, cash was probably tight, and they hadn't spent too much. Maybe he'd pay for something else later in his visit.

"Hey, let's stop in that Wal-Mart we passed!" Hank said. "Sue Ann and me, we go there a lot on a Saturday night—they have these specials."

"Sure," Karen agreed. "I've never been in the evening."

She was surprised at the crowds in the store, whole families with strollers, old ladies with fists full of coupons, and employees wearing bright red vests proclaiming "Ask me! I can help!"

Hank began filling their cart. A huge Florida T-shirt for himself, a case of dog food, and can of motor oil.

"Welcome, Wal-Mart shoppers!" The loudspeaker interrupted whatever conversation Karen had been attempting to make with Sue Ann while Hank shopped. "Free paring knives available at the red table by aisle 42!"

Hank turned abruptly, cart nearly colliding with a gaggle of teenagers who were posing in sunglasses for each other. "Let's go get one of those knives," he said.

The three headed to aisle 42 and found it crowded already. A woman in a red jumpsuit was brusquely shoving carts away from a platform. "People need to be able to reach up," she said. When she had arranged the crowd into a thick knot, she jumped up onto the platform and positioned herself behind a table.

"Before I give out the paring knives, I have something to tell you about. This is my job, so please be patient. You'll find I can talk very fast." To prove her point, the woman switched to the speed of an Isuzu commercial.

"This is the Super-Tough Stainless Steel Surgical Blade knife, you've probably seen it on TV." She held aloft a long knife with a deeply serrated edge. The onlookers raised their eyes respectfully as she began to enumerate its benefits. "It's beveled as you can see, and the edge never dulls. I've been using this same one for months and it's just the same as a new blade, see, this one next to it is brand-new and you can't tell the difference." She turned to show everyone in the crowd the identical knives.

She held up a tomato and passed it over the knife a few times, allowing paper-thin slices to fall onto the table. "The Super-Tough knife gives you a slice of tomato you can see through. Why, some of the restaurants around here have been using the same tomato for six weeks!" Hank's mouth dropped open as he watched raptly.

"If I dropped this knife onto my wrist, it would go right to the bone!" she added. Hank shuddered.

"If you've seen this knife on TV, you know it's $39.95. But when we do these demos in the stores, we're authorized to sell two for the price of one! You can get one for yourself and still have one to use for a Christmas gift." Karen tried to picture Lucy opening her gift under the tree and finding the cruelly serrated blade in front of her.

Hank looked at Karen with eyes ablaze. "We can both have one!"

"No, that's fine, Hank, I really have all the knives I can use, so...." Hank ignored her.

"Ever try to cut a loaf of bread with an ordinary knife?" the saleswoman went on. To prove her point, she stuck the point of a non-serrated knife into a loaf of white bread, a tough loaf that appeared to have seen plenty of use. The knife compressed the loaf to a pancake immediately. "Ruins the bread. Now with the Super-Tough Stainless Steel Surgical Blade, you can make a neat slice of any thinness." The bread resumed its original shape, and she showed the superior capabilities of the serrated knife by neatly removing a few thin slices and holding them up for the crowd's approval.

"And just for tonight, if you buy within the next half hour, I can let you have two for half-price; yes, folks, two knives, each worth $39.95, for the price of only $19.95. And I can add this handy juicer." She whipped out a small green plastic device and stuck it into an orange. Juice flowed into a glass. "But the offer's only good for another half-hour."

People began waving credit cards and bills at the woman. Still she continued her talk.

"Don't think it's cheap just because it's inexpensive. Ask any chef, they'll tell you the Super-Tough Stainless Steel Surgical Blade is the only one they'll use—if they can get one. This is a limited offer, so don't wait."

Hank joined the crowd of eager purchasers, pushing aside an elderly woman to put his twenty-dollar bill into the hand of the saleswoman. He returned with his prize and presented one to Karen. "Bet you can use this orange gizmo here in Florida with all these oranges they grow here!" he said. There was no point to protest. She thanked him and put the knife into the cart along with the free paring knife she'd listened so long to earn.

* * * *

Karen and Hank and Sue Ann soon fell into a routine, which suggested to Karen that they planned to stay a long time. She rehearsed casual questions like, "So how long do you plan to stay?" No, maybe it should be "So how long *can* you stay?" Maybe she should say, "When do you have to head back north?" How about "When do you have to start job-hunting?" Nothing seemed right, and there was the matter of timing. Timing was everything. You couldn't ask a question like that unless it was the right moment. She looked for hints in their conversation, but all she picked up were things Hank wanted to do in Naples.

Meanwhile, she heard nothing from Curly. She thought he was probably waiting for her to call, to tell him her guests were gone, to resume where they left off, but there was nothing she could do. She couldn't call. She felt that terrible sense of letting go, of the incomplete, even comical, ending to an otherwise golden evening when Hank's truck appeared in the parking lot. But there was no way she could bring Curly along with her cousin—an evening with Curly and Hank would be like mixing Kevin Costner and Willie Nelson.

Hank and Sue Ann woke early, veterans of many years of blue-collar jobs. Hank walked Kaiser first thing, while Karen explained to Junior that he'd have yet another day in the bedroom. Each day, Karen dutifully showed them around, taking them for a day at the beach or a walk out the Naples Pier.

Hank learned that you could fish on the pier without a license, so he spent a day with Kaiser trying his luck, while Karen and Sue Ann browsed in the upscale shoppes in Naples. Since Hank had taken sandwiches and a can of beer for his lunch on the pier, the two women stopped at Tommy Bahama's outdoor café for lunch. "Looks expensive," Sue Ann said.

"It's not, and besides, it's my treat," Karen told her.

They settled back to watch the passersby over iced tea while they waited for their salads. Sue Ann gaped at a woman dressed in lemon yellow from head to toe, a man sporting two Afghan hounds on short leather leashes, and a couple carrying at least six shopping bags, jostling and jouncing as they made their way along the crowded sidewalk.

"You're doing OK by yourself, aren't you?" Sue Ann asked Karen.

"Yes, at first I was really scared. I even thought of asking Tom to come back to me because I was so afraid. Well, he remarried right away and I thought I'd be a bag lady without him, but I did just fine. I found I didn't need a man to earn a living. It's amazing what you can do when you have to"

"Sometimes I wish I was on my own," Sue Ann said.

"You and Hank aren't getting along?"

Sue Ann waited a moment to answer, while the waiter placed their salads in front of them and offered a twist from the peppermill. "It's not so much that," she said, "Sometimes I just want things quiet. My own apartment with my own TV and the closets kept neat the way I like it and no Kaiser and nobody's underwear laying on the floor and cooking what I want to eat. It's not really Hank's fault, he doesn't hit me a lot, only when I've done something to provoke him, but he's kind of a bear."

"Hank *hits* you? Karen asked. "Sue Ann, this is way out of my business, but no woman ever does anything that justifies a man hitting her."

"He doesn't really mean it, because he always apologizes after. Anybody asks me about a bruise or anything, I just tell them I took a fall. It's nobody's business. Hank's under a lot of stress, what with jobs coming and going. He loves me, in his way." Sue Ann turned from Karen to concentrate on her salad, carefully cutting the tails off the shrimp.

"Sue Ann, nobody's way of loving, really loving, includes hitting," Karen said.

Sue Ann looked up. "It's not like it happens every day. And we've had a good life, if you look at it all. The two boys are grown now, and they turned out to be great kids. Wayne just got into the Teamsters, so he's set for life. I wish we'd have known you when Paulie got married. You could have come to the wedding. Now I can't wait till we have grandchildren."

Karen reached over to touch Sue Ann's hand. "We've missed a lot of years of being family. I know Hank doesn't have any more cousins or uncles than I do. We were always afraid of Hank's father, John, who was a heavy drinker, I'm sure you know."

"Hank doesn't hardly talk about his father, but I know he scared Hank a lot when he was a kid, he could hear his parents fighting in the night. During the day and when he had a buzz on he was a real happy drunk, but at night, I guess he turned into somebody else. He died before I met Hank." Sue Ann accepted a refill of her iced tea and looked up at Karen, who was remembering the stories of John's cirrhosis, and the stories about the bottles found hidden all over the house and garage.

"Does Hank drink too?" she asked. She hadn't observed him going for much more than the occasional beer, but she was afraid the family curse would devolve on her cousin. Maybe it was only the outward signs, the show of violence, the harming of a servile wife, that Hank had inherited.

"No, he doesn't. He works hard, has a couple beers with the guys at the Lodge on Friday night, but that's all. I guess he doesn't want to turn out like his Dad."

"I'm sure he won't," Karen said, feeling none of the confidence she was trying to exude.

The two walked slowly back to the pier where Hank was cleaning his catch at the benches and tables provided for the purpose. Karen noted that he had laid aside his new Wal-Mart knife—perhaps it was too big for the job of cutting into the small fish he'd caught. As each fisherman threw the discarded fish parts over the rail, a dozen huge pelicans bobbing in the water fought for the snack. Just as Karen and Sue returned, Hank was shooing off a big bird that had flown up to the pier to compete for Hank's prize. Hank was winning, but he'd drawn a crowd of pelicans and gulls as he worked.

"I'll clean the damn things at home!" he shouted over the cawing. Karen did not look forward to this prospect, but thought she'd better get Hank out of there as soon as possible.

* * * *

Karen was running out of tourist attractions for the ebullient Hank and his patient wife, so she finally considered the Wonder Gardens. You couldn't really visit Bonita Springs without seeing the Wonder Gardens, and

Hank had been reading from the billboards each time they drove on Old Route 41.

It was impossible to leave Kaiser out in the car during their visit, so they secured him in the guest room of Karen's apartment, with Junior's door equally tightly closed. Karen drove with Hank in the front seat. "Kash 'n Karry. Dollar Central. Bank of America," Hank read as they drove through the center of town.

"Lot of Puerto Ricans here in Florida," Hank observed. Karen winced.

"Most of the Hispanic people here come from Cuba or Mexico or Guatemala," she corrected him.

"Oh sure," Hank said. "All the Puerto Ricans go to New York."

Karen parked and the three walked to the ticket booth where she bought three tickets. The ticket-taker must have been new, because she didn't react to Karen's presence. She led them to the start of the tour, a huge 80-year-old crocodile. "Big Joe here was found by a fisherman, caught in a net, in 1936," the guide explained. "He's been livin' in this pond all that time. 14 ½ feet long." The animal appeared to be completely inert, even to the algae growing on its back, until the guide gave him a nudge with a very long pole. Big Joe snapped at him, opening enormous jaws. Karen saw Charlie in her mind's eye.

Hank was completely absorbed in the animals and in the guide's spiel about them. Karen had heard it so many times she felt she could deliver it herself.

As they passed the tiny Florida deer, Karen saw Curly out of the corner of her eye. He was upending a huge sack of dog food into the flamingo trough. Flamingos derive their pink color from eating shellfish, but for reasons of thrift, the Wonder Gardens had produced the same effect by sprinkling paprika on dog food.

She began picking at her nail polish, looking away from him and then back at him. She rehearsed a number of things she could say, but she was unable to choke out even a simple greeting.

His task finished, he looked up and caught her staring at him. "Karen," he said, heading toward her as the group moved on to the turtle pond.

"Curly. How have you been?" she asked awkwardly, not knowing where to put her hands and arms.

"I'm just hanging out," he said. "I see you're still entertaining your relations…how long has it been?"

"Two weeks tomorrow," she replied with a sigh. "I wish they'd show some sign of wanting to go home. You'd think Hank would have to go look for a job, but he doesn't say a thing about it, and when I ask, he tells me not to worry."

"He's doing pretty well living off you," Curly said as he folded the empty dog food bags.

"Curly, this isn't how I wanted things to be," Karen ventured.

"That's up to you, isn't it?" he said and turned back down the path away from the tour.

Chapter 9

Karen brought her guests back to the apartment, planning to cook the kind of hearty dinner Hank enjoyed—meat loaf, baked potatoes, and a salad. She felt a wave of weariness from the day. She'd had no break from days of taking them places, arranging for their meals and comforts, and always staying "up." She wanted nothing more than to curl up with Junior and a book for the rest of the afternoon, but she knew they had to walk Kaiser, get ready for dinner, and keep up the steady talk, talk, talk.

Kaiser bounded out of the bedroom where he'd been imprisoned. "Hey, let's get your leash and go for a walk, Big Guy!" Hank said. The dog jumped up on him and ran around in delirious circles. It was clear that Kaiser needed more exercise than he was getting while confined to Karen's tiny guest bedroom.

Karen wanted to change her shoes for sandals, so she opened the door to her bedroom. That's all it took. Kaiser streaked past her and lunged for the bed, where Junior had been sleeping. Before Junior could dive under the bed where he'd be safe from the huge dog, Kaiser caught the cat in his jaws, crouched on the bed and began to shake him from side to side. Junior didn't have a moment to defend himself with his claws.

Karen was insane with rage. She screamed and hit the dog with all her might, pounding her fists into his head, and finally pried the cat out of his jaws. Junior lay limp on the bedspread, soft fur spattered with blood, a gash in his chest where his little white ruff had been. The dog now began snarling at her, sinking his teeth into her arm.

"HANK!" Karen screamed. "Get this dog!" Hank raced into the bedroom and pulled the dog by the collar. "Get him out of this house now. Go! Now!" Hank pulled Kaiser off the bed and the two slunk out of the bedroom.

Karen stroked Junior's bloody fur. He was still breathing raggedly and moving his white paws. She took the carrier down from the closet shelf, stuffed a pillowcase into it, and gently placed Junior into the carrier.

She brushed past the snarling dog and her cousin. "Sue Ann, come with me." Sue Ann opened the door so Karen could move the bulky carrier through it without bumping the cat. "You drive," Karen ordered as they got into the garage. She handed Sue Ann the keys and sat in the back seat with the carrier. She used her cell phone to call the vet.

Karen gave directions to the veterinary clinic, and Sue Ann dropped her off at the door. Fortunately the staff was ready for them and took the carrier out of Karen's hands.

Only then could she break down. She sobbed insanely, picturing her trusting cat in her arms, the day she'd found the terrified kitten and given him his first bath, the loud purr he started up as soon as he settled into her lap. The veterinary technician finally called her into one of the offices. Sue Ann had parked the car, so she came along. She took Karen's hand in hers.

"The doctor is with your cat now," the technician said. "He might be able to save the little fellow, but he can't be sure. It's going to be expensive."

"I don't care what it costs," Karen said. "Don't spare anything to save Junior."

"He's in good health, a little overweight, but he's not young. There's no way to say if he'll come through. You should go home. Dr. Peterson will call you when he's finished. There's nothing you can do here. But you might want to report the dog to the authorities."

"The dog will be out of the state of Florida by tonight," Karen replied.

Karen and Sue Ann walked out to the parking lot in silence. Karen drove home, slowly and without speaking. There would be no further polite chat, even to the bewildered Sue Ann.

Karen saw Kaiser tied to the pickup truck in the parking lot. She opened the door to the apartment and looked for Hank. She flung the door of the guest room open and barged in.

"Get out. I want you gone. This was a mistake and now I may have lost the dearest companion of my life."

Karen wasn't sure what had come over her, but she needed to continue. "I tried to be tolerant of that vicious dog not because of any affection for him—or for that matter for you—but because of some dream of family. We have a small genetic connection, and a few childhood memories, which I exaggerated for that dream, but Hank, we have nothing in common. Nothing. It's time for you to go. Long past."

Hank was speechless for the first time in his long visit as if listening to a stranger. Sue Ann wiped tears away with her fingers as she listened.

Finally Hank spoke up, softly for once. "Listen, Karen, I know the dog is aggressive, but I had no idea he'd try to kill your cat. I never thought of it. But look at it this way—you can get another cat if this one doesn't pull through, but you can't get another cousin."

"Get out," Karen said. "If I'd had a lingering doubt about you, which I don't, that would have killed it."

"I don't understand," Hank said. "You're just upset. A good night's sleep and we can...."

"In the morning I will wake up alone in this apartment, if I sleep at all, which is unlikely. You will wake up somewhere else, and I hope that will be many miles from here." To emphasize her point, she picked up the suitcase standing behind the door, opened it on the unmade bed, and began to throw Hank and Sue Ann's clothing into it. Sue Ann quickly took over the job.

"I believe Sue Ann understands me," Karen said, still looking at Hank. Karen felt a moment's pain for Sue Ann, but there was nothing she could do for a woman who chose to stay with a man like Hank. Sue Ann would have to make her own way.

Karen left the room and headed to the bedroom and closed the door firmly but quietly behind her. Next she confronted the stains from Junior's wound. Sobbing helplessly, she took the bedspread off the bed and tossed it on the floor. She stripped off her bloody clothes and threw them onto the bedspread, changing into a clean nightgown. She would deal with the pile of laundry some other time. She saw Junior's little catnip mouse on the floor and picked it up, crushing it in her fist, willing strength and health and wholeness to her cat, praying with all her heart.

After a while Karen heard the door close. She blessed Sue Ann, who must have been able to persuade Hank that they should just leave without making another scene. Now she was alone and she needed to do something to get through the night. She wandered through her apartment, noting the mess Hank and Sue Ann had left in the guest room, but unable to deal with it now. Books, food, television—nothing appealed to her. She couldn't call Lucy because she'd left her cell phone in the car, and she had to leave the home phone line open for the vet's call. There was nothing to do but watch night fall.

Finally the phone rang and Karen jumped to answer it. "This is Dr. Peterson," the vet said. "Junior is resting and I hope he's healing. He's got a 50-50 chance. I'm going to leave him here tonight so one of the techs can watch him and call me if I'm needed. If you like, you can come over—just ring the bell—the cat won't be conscious but they'll let you in and you can see him. If he makes it through tonight, he'll have a good chance, but I need to tell you he's in very serious condition and I can't be sure he'll survive."

"Tell me about his injury," Karen said.

"It's a condition called pneumothorax—the chest cavity is punctured, so the lungs can't get enough pressure to expand and contract. The cat can't breathe. We've put in a tube to do his breathing for him, and the hope is that the chest wall will heal and he can start breathing on his own in a day or two. I've seen cases where animals recover from this."

"I'll be right there," Karen said. She dressed again and drove to the clinic where the attendant showed her to Junior's cage. The poor cat had had his white ruff shaved off, and an ugly tube protruded from his open mouth. The puncture wounds appeared red and ugly on the shaved skin. But Karen was heartened to see his chest rise and fall, however artificially.

"Like some coffee?" the tech offered. "It will keep you awake."

112

"No, thanks," Karen answered. "I don't think I have a chance of falling asleep."

"Poor Junior was hurt pretty bad," the young man said. "I've never seen one like that. But Dr. Peterson is the best—if anybody could save Junior, he can."

"What do you think, from watching him?" Karen asked.

"He looks good, really he does."

The tech went on to the other cages, where animals were more restless and noisy. Junior slept on. Eventually it was morning, and the clinic staff started to arrive.

Dr. Peterson came in and smiled when he saw Karen. "You spent the night with him? Let's see how he's doing!"

The doctor moved closer to the cat and probed the ugly wounds on his little chest. "He's hanging in there!" he said. Karen prayed as she never had before for Junior.

Chapter 10

Heartened by the prospects for Junior's survival, and hoping this would be her last day without him, Karen returned home alone. She threw her T-shirt and shorts on the floor and fell into bed. Ignoring all the tasks she had to do, she finally fell asleep. But after only a couple of hours she stirred, and the horror of the previous day snapped back into her consciousness. Her mind's eye saw the limp body of her dear cat, and she replayed her speech to Hank. There would be no more sleep.

Could she hope ever to have her little cat back in her arms again? Of course she'd always outlived her pets, but none had ever died violently. And if she'd only listened to Curly, she could have prevented the tragedy. Curly could see right away that Kaiser was bad news, but she wouldn't hear of any criticism of her *family*. Could she put the time with Hank and Sue Ann behind her for good? Would she ever have the happy retirement she'd dreamed of for so many years?

She dressed quickly and made a thermos of hot tea to carry with her back to Dr. Peterson's office. She was just pouring some orange juice when the phone rang.

"This is Dr. Husey," the voice announced.

Husey. Husey. Oh! From another memory, from another world, the diminutive Lee County coroner came to mind. "Yes," Karen replied.

"Did you know a Henry Sinclair?" he asked.

"He's my cousin," Karen told him, "but he's no longer with me. He's on his way back to New Jersey. He left late last night, with his wife, Sue Ann."

"You'd better come down to my office at the hospital. And if you're planning on not coming, we can send someone to pick you up."

"I'm very busy this morning," Karen said. "If you have any further questions about Craig Walters, I can answer them another day, but I'm in the midst of a family emergency."

"You need to be here inside of an hour," Husey said. "We need kin to identify Sinclair's body."

"Body?" Karen gasped. "Body?"

Husey paused a moment. "If you really don't know, Hank was stabbed to death sometime very early this morning. We found him alone. We don't know anything about his family except that he had your name and phone number written on a map on the dashboard of his pickup truck, and your name was familiar to me because it turns up every couple of weeks in connection with somebody who died for some reason or another. Now are you going to get down here or do I have to send somebody from the P.D.to bring you here?"

"I'll be there," Karen said. She drove erratically toward the hospital where they'd taken Craig after his terrible accident.

This time the coroner's receptionist ushered Karen into his office right away. Dr. Husey, now wearing a white coat, jumped up from his desk and said, "Let's go." The two walked to the elevator and rode it down to the basement floor in silence. As they exited, she saw a sign marked COUNTY MORGUE and shuddered. She knew they existed, of course, but she'd hoped never to see one. A uniformed policeman rose from a chair near the door and joined them.

She wasn't prepared for the smell of formaldehyde in the cold, clammy room. The doctor opened a drawer and pulled out a body draped with a sheet. When he slowly pulled the sheet down to reveal the head, Karen could see that it was Hank, unmistakably, now a cold gray. The coroner lifted Hank's double chins and Karen could see the dark, wine-colored smear of congealed blood at his throat.

"That your cousin?" Dr. Husey asked.

Karen took a quick step backward, away from the ugly scene. She started as she bumped into a cart of surgical instruments behind her. "Yes, that's Hank.

Henry Sinclair. Where is his wife, Sue Ann? She was with him when they left."

"I don't know, but I'm asking the sergeant here to take you in for questioning." Husey motioned to the policeman and turned to walk out without another word.

The sergeant approached the dumfounded Karen and began to speak. "I'm Sgt. Hoff," he said. "This doesn't have to be hard if you'll do what I tell you," he said.

Karen couldn't absorb it all but at some point he showed her the cuffs he was holding in his hand. She shook her head and closed her eyes. The man propelled her by the elbow into the parking garage. He took her purse, put her into the back seat of the police car, and closed the door behind her.

Separated from the front of the car by a grille and a glass plate, Karen felt a moment of claustrophobia, as she tried to breathe in spite of the smell of many old cigarettes. She leaned her head against the window and tried to look out it as the car crawled through morning traffic. Finally they arrived at the police station, and Hoff opened the door and held her arm as she got out. The two walked past the crowded foyer and upstairs to a small cubicle, which must have been his office. He motioned to the plastic chair facing his desk. As she took her seat, he pressed a button on his telephone console.

The two faced each other in silence until another man appeared, bringing his own plastic chair into the crowded cubicle. Hoff indicated the newcomer, who was wearing a gray business suit and scuffed shoes. "This here's Frank Nicolo, from Homicide."

Homicide! Even with all the unimaginable deaths that she'd faced in such a short time, the word had never come up, even in her middle-of-the-night thoughts. As Nicolo shook her hand, she wondered how much business a homicide detective could possibly have in their quiet community.

"Maybe if we talk we can clear this up and you can go home," Nicolo said.

"I hope so," Karen said gratefully.

"Gum?" Nicolo asked, offering her a packet of Spearmint.

"No, thanks," Karen said.

"What was your relationship to Henry Sinclair?" Nicolo asked.

"Well, he was a cousin, but we weren't close. I hadn't seen him in many years, and he came here so we could get acquainted again. But actually, I threw him out last night, told him to leave." As soon as she said that, she realized her mistake.

"So there was a conflict between you?" Nicolo asked.

"He had a big vicious dog, and it attacked my cat. I'm very attached to the cat, and it broke my heart. I realized Hank—that's what we call him—and I didn't really have anything in common, except some time together when we were children. And he'd been staying with me a long time, so I just got fed up. I told him to leave. Then I went to the veterinary clinic and I stayed there for hours, they'll tell you I did." She scribbled the name of the veterinarian on a pad.

"Dr. Husey says two of your previous house guests also died while they were visiting you." A Charles Townsend and a Craig Walters. Both died inside of a month. Accidents. That's quite a coincidence."

"Yes, it is," Karen said, finally grasping where the detective was going with this. "But they *were* accidents, incredible as it seems. One was eaten by crocodiles because he fell into the pond…"

"Were you fed up with them too?" Nicolo asked.

"No, I have a lot of house guests, as we all do down here, but I wasn't exactly *fed up*." She realized she was talking too fast.

"Have you ever seen this knife?" Nicolo interrupted. From his briefcase, he produced the Super-Tough Stainless Steel Surgical Blade knife in a plastic bag.

"Yes! It's mine! At least it *could* be mine. Hank bought two of them at Wal-Mart while he was visiting. He kept one and he gave one to me. You can check my apartment to see if mine is there," Karen said.

"OK, Hoff, take a note that we don't need a warrant," Nicolo said to the sergeant. "Give us your house key." Karen fumbled in her purse and drew out her key ring, fingers shaking.

Nicolo turned his attention back to the knife. "It's the weapon used on Sinclair. Nasty blade, isn't it? Looks as if a person who wasn't as strong as Sinclair could kill him using a blade like this."

"You can look for fingerprints!" Karen shouted. "You just took mine a few minutes ago, and you can see that they're not on this blade."

"This blade and the knife handle have been wiped clean," Nicolo said. "The killer thought of that. But we're checking for prints on the truck."

"We've been going places together all week, sometimes in his truck. But I didn't kill him. I was at the veterinary clinic till the staff arrived in the morning, and then I came home exhausted. I did ask Hank to leave, and we did have a conflict, after all his dog nearly killed my cat, but I wouldn't have killed him!"

"We found the dog in the pickup. It was a pretty nasty dog, you're right about that, tried to take a nip out of Hoff here, and we've taken the mutt to the pound. If somebody doesn't claim him in three days, he could be put down," Nicolo said, watching Karen as he spoke.

"The only other person who could clear this up is Hank's wife Sue Ann," Karen said, ignoring the fate of the detested Kaiser. "Why wasn't she with him? They were together all the time. I can't imagine her not being with him. You just have to find her. She's probably afraid, but she can tell you what happened."

Karen had read somewhere that the spouse is always the first suspect.

"Didn't they tell you where they were going?" Nicolo asked.

"No, I didn't ask. I didn't really care. I guess I must have thought they'd be headed back to New Jersey. They didn't have a lot of money. Hank had just been laid off from his job."

"This is all we have to ask you," Nicolo said. Karen wondered who "we" were, because the sergeant had said scarcely a word. "I'm afraid our talk has raised more questions than it's answered."

The two left Karen alone in Hoff's cluttered office for a few moments. She looked around at the stacks of papers and began to fear that this had become serious beyond her ability to fix. She prayed quickly for help.

When Nicolo re-entered, he had a pair of handcuffs on his belt. "We're placing you under arrest for the murder of Henry Sinclair. Our investigation shows you had motive, a weapon, and opportunity to do this killing and return to the veterinarian's office, where the assistant tells me you came in covered with blood."

"But it was Junior's blood! The dog had nearly killed him, torn his throat apart. I didn't bother to change because I wanted to be by his side. You can run tests on the blood—my clothes are still on my bedroom floor! You can't arrest me for this!"

"Yes, we can. We can't take the chance that you'll flee the state. You'll be in custody until such time as you appear before a judge. You're innocent until you're proven guilty, and maybe we can't prove our case against you, and then you're not a suspect any more. Hoff, read her her rights."

Just as she'd seen on the TV shows Tom loved, the sergeant recited the Miranda rights. One word stood out from the familiar speech: *attorney*. Everything she had said had gotten her into more trouble, rather than clearing up the misunderstanding, and she needed help. She decided to take her right to an attorney seriously, and to offer no further information to the two police officers.

Hoff led her to the elevator and down a flight to the detention center, mercifully omitting the handcuffs that still jangled at his waist. He led her through a series of procedures she'd only seen on television—fingerprinting, searching, and photographing her at two angles. Karen couldn't have felt more naked and exposed. A woman attendant led her toward a row of barred cells, but paused beside a wall-mounted telephone. Karen remembered something about making one phone call.

She dialed Lucy's number. How would she ever explain what had happened? What could Lucy do to help anyway? After four rings, the machine switched on. "I'm in the Lee County Detention Center. I'm not sure where it is because I came in a police car. I'm under arrest." She paused. There was no way to explain and she lost the power of words.

"I need help. I need a lawyer. They think I killed Hank. And I need for you to find out about Junior. Please." Karen knew her message would be baffling, but she prayed Lucy would come and she could explain.

Would even Lucy think she had killed Hank? Where was Sue Ann?

"That doesn't count, does it? She wasn't home?" Karen asked the attendant, who hesitated a moment and then said, "go ahead." Karen dialed the Wonder Gardens, amazed that she'd remembered the number after calling so few times.

After a moment, Curly was found and brought to the phone. "Aubusson here," he said abruptly.

"Curly, it's Karen. I'm in the county jail. They think I murdered Hank." Her voice broke and she waited for him to respond. Any response at all. Of course he was silent, absorbing the double shock that she was calling him in the first place after their long awkward time apart, and then that this quiet woman was an accused killer.

"What jail? Where?" he asked.

"Lee County Detention Center. I'm not even sure where it is because the police car brought me here. Please, find me."

"I'll be there," he said and hung up.

The attendant led Karen to a cell and gently pushed her inside. Karen's throat closed as the door clanked shut behind her. She fought to keep breathing.

She sat on the hard bed, the lower of two bunks. It occurred to her that she was glad there was no one else in the cell. What would she do? Where was Sue Ann? What had happened to Hank? The noise coming from the other cells prevented her from thinking through her situation.

With nothing to do but wait for help, she lay on the bed. Looking at the slats under the bunk above her, she prayed. She'd heard that God never gives you more than you can take, but if that was true, she was at her limit.

It seemed as if hours passed before a guard unlocked her cell and ordered her to go to the interview room. Terrible visions came to her mind from TV crime shows. She followed him to a spare-looking room with a table, three chairs, note pads, pencils, and an ashtray. The guard gave her no explanation of why she was being moved to this room, but in a moment, Curly appeared at the door.

She ran to him and threw her arms around him. The guard pulled her away. "You can visit with supervision." Karen sputtered out the astonishing story, conscious that the guard was listening, but knowing she had nothing to hide. Curly held her hand, not interrupting until she had finished the whole disjointed narrative.

"They can't hold you on such flimsy evidence. They don't have a case—you admitted to owning a knife like the one that killed Hank, you admitted to having a conflict with him, the vet's assistant said you were covered with blood, and a lot of other people have died in the last couple of months—that's all circumstance and hearsay. People don't spend jail time for that. You need a lawyer, one who will sue them blind. You need Junior. You need to find Sue Ann. I'm going now. I'll be back."

"Sue Ann will be the answer to all this. He's been hitting her, she told me. She had a better motive than I did for killing him—mousy little thing that she is, maybe she finally got up the courage to fight back. It happens. Find Sue Ann. *Please* find Sue Ann."

Curly kissed her on the cheek, and signaled to the guard. They walked the few steps back to Karen's cell, where she was locked up again. She watched Curly's lanky body taking long strides, until she could no longer see him through the bars. Finally she dissolved into tears on her mildewed blanket.

Chapter 11

A cardboard tray appeared at Karen's cell with a meal of a large roll and some luncheon meat inside. She found a can of juice and an apple with a large brown spot on the side. There was no silverware.

She blanketed the sandwich with salt and pepper so it would taste like something, and started to munch on the unappetizing fare, realizing she hadn't eaten since her dinner with Hank and Sue Ann Saturday night. And that was nearly 24 hours ago. Where was Sue Ann? Was she so terrorized by seeing Hank's murder that she'd run away? Was she murdered too? If so, her body would have been found with Hank's. Or, more likely, had that mousy woman finally decided she'd had enough of Hank's casual cruelty? Could she have had the strength to kill this huge man?

Before she could finish, she heard footsteps and the welcome voice of Lucy.

"Karen, Karen!" Lucy reached through the bars and stroked Karen's hair. The attendant unlocked the door and walked the two women toward the interview room.

Again, Karen told the story of Kaiser's vicious attack, Junior's grave injury, her own ultimatum to Hank, and her unimaginable—and probably illegal—arrest the next day.

"I'll drive over to Dr. Peterson's. I wish I could stay with you, but things have to be done. I have a key to your place. If I can get Junior home, I'll stay with him." Karen knew Lucy was right but she needed a friend in this cold and harsh place. Lucy's practicality was exactly the right approach, but Karen needed comforting.

"I know, I know. But I'm so lonely here." Karen broke down.

"The best thing we can do for you is to save your cat and get you out of here. I'll be back, Karen, I'll be back."

Sunday was the longest day she could remember. The book cart had a few offerings of mysteries and romance novels, but nothing Karen cared to read. Still she plowed through a couple of them, ignoring the noise of singing, radios, and calls to and from the other cells. She was allowed out to the day room, but found only a blaring television there. The other women argued furiously over the choice of programs, and Karen knew she wouldn't fare well in a conflict with this crowd.

The highlight of each day was mealtime, because it broke the monotony, but the food was consistently gray, tepid, and stale. She wondered where Lucy and Curly were, and especially where Sue Ann was. Finding Sue Ann was the key to getting her out of this place. She agonized over Junior, praying for him to recover without her presence and encouragement

On Sunday night, the cells began to fill with more women who had clearly been reveling—perhaps at a price—all weekend. Just as she thought she'd escaped the fate of being assigned a roommate, her cell door clanked open. Two attendants flanked a hugely obese woman dressed from neck to foot in a flowered silk caftan. Adding several inches to her height was a matching turban, anchored by outsize hoop earrings. As the attendants shoved her into Karen's cell, she tripped on her absurdly high heels. Karen caught her just before she fell. The woman scarcely noticed as she turned to shake her fists at the attendants. Rows of bracelets jangled and rings flashed from every finger. Waves of My Sin perfume filled the cell.

"Arrested in my own church! Right during a prayer! God won't forget what you've done, no way!" she shouted.

The attendants turned and left. With the loss of that audience, the woman noticed Karen. "Who are you?" she asked.

"I'm Karen Sinclair. And who are you?"

"I'm Lavinia Willingham, known to my followers as Queen Lavinia. That would be the best thing for you to call me," the woman replied, stretching out on the lower bunk.

"I've been sleeping on the lower bunk, Lavinia," Karen said, balking at the idea of calling this ridiculous woman 'Queen.'

"I can't get up there to the top," the woman replied imperiously. You're younger and you'll have to sleep up there."

Karen could see her point. Between the shoes and the voluminous dress, the woman would trip on the first step up the ladder, if the ladder didn't collapse under her bulk. So she reluctantly put her bag and her bedding on the upper bunk, saying goodbye to the halcyon days of a private cell.

"Why are you here?" Karen asked.

"It's all lies. My lawyers will straighten it out by morning, I'm sure. I've been accused of fraud, of taking money given to my church. I'm a minister, you see, from the Church of True Happiness in Fort Myers. The cops came and got me during evening prayers, can you imagine?"

Fortunately Queen Lavinia showed no interest in asking about Karen's story. "I have a parish of 200 believers, and we understand that God wants us to have prosperity. Every week we affirm together, 'I love money and money loves me!'" she continued.

"They say somebody informed on me. No way! They just can't stand my success; they're always looking in my books and sending the IRS people around. I can't be bothered to be an accountant, writing down every penny. I'm too busy preaching the gospel of happiness! You belong to a church?" she asked.

At any other time of her life, Karen might have laughed at the prospect of being evangelized by the Church of True Happiness, but her sense of humor was stretched a bit thin just now. "I'm a Lutheran," Karen said, feeling somehow dowdy, like a character from a Garrison Keillor monologue.

"We got lots of people used to be Lutheran, girl. But it wasn't giving them happiness."

"Well, I guess it's all in how you define 'happy,'" Karen ventured.

"Are you happy?" the ridiculous woman asked, removing her turban and revealing a great deal of brown hair flattened to her head.

"Well, not in this cell I'm not," Karen replied. "And I don't think you are either!"

"I'm always happy. Happiness is a choice. You can choose to be happy right here in this jail cell. I'm happy right now because I know I'm going to get out of this mess. I'm going to be victorious. I need to affirm 'happiness is my right.' Come on, girl, affirm with me: 'happiness is my right.'"

Karen said, "I don't run to affirmations much, but I think I'll get into my bunk and read. So good night to you."

Karen wasn't a bit tired, but she needed to terminate the conversation right now. She glanced at her watch and found it was only 9:15. Too late for a visit from anyone she cared about, but far too early to fall asleep. She opened one of the books she'd taken from the cart. From the bunk below came chanting. "Happiness is my right, happiness is my right."

Eventually Queen Lavinia drifted off to sleep, but it wasn't much of an improvement because loud snoring replaced the chanting. Somehow Karen got through the night and woke to the clanking and talk around her. After another tray meal, this time a synthetic-looking Danish pastry wrapped in cellophane with a carton of orange juice and a mug of coffee, Karen readied herself for news. After wolfing down her meal, Queen Lavinia began adorning herself with the jewels she'd stored under her pillow. Karen hoped she'd left the perfume at home before her arrest.

Before long, in answer to Karen's own prayer, Curly arrived. "Nice to see this quiet little gal has a boyfriend," Queen Lavinia said, giving Curly a pathetically seductive once-over.

Somehow Curly managed to arrange for a private interview room for them to talk. Although the attendant was watching them, he took time for a long kiss and a serious hug. Karen drew in strength from his arms.

'Junior is home, first of all," Curly told her. "Lucy is staying with him. He's really doing great. They said that as soon as they got the fluid out of his chest cavity, and the punctures healed up, he'd start breathing on his own again, and that's what's happening, in only a couple of days. Lucy is pampering him to pieces—last I saw she was cooking up fresh salmon for the little guy.

"But the court business is not such good news," Curly went on. "They rejected the argument that you'd been arrested illegally. Then they set bail, but then the judge decided he wouldn't allow it, because it's a murder case and you don't have family here to keep you in town."

"It's trying to be part of a family that got me into this mess in the first place," Karen observed. "Anyway, does that mean I have to stay in this cell until my trial?"

"Yes, I'm afraid it does. And it's going to take your attorney a long time to assemble some kind of defense."

"My attorney?" Karen asked.

"Yes, who do you think was telling the judge you shouldn't have been arrested in the first place? I found a guy from a friend at work. The friend's brother was accused of rape after a date and...it's a long story. Anyway, the lawyer got him off and he's willing to take your case. He'll be here later today to talk to you. His name's William Daly."

"Won't you come home, Bill Daly?" Karen sang.

"I didn't think you had anything funny left in you," Curly said, "But if you can't laugh at that roommate, you're finished. Her story is all over the local papers. She's been ripping off this church for months, ordering her followers to steal jewelry for her and fencing it in Tampa while she preaches that prosperity begins with giving—to her."

"Curly, where is Sue Ann? We can clear this up in a minute if we can find Sue Ann. She must have been with him."

"They tell me they're looking for her," Curly replied. "But it doesn't sound like a high priority for them, since she's probably out of the area. They're in touch with New Jersey State Police, but nobody has any news yet. I think I'd do better to try to find her myself."

"But your job!" Karen said.

"I've got some time off. But it means I might not be able to visit for a while."

Karen tried to hide her dismay, but Curly wasn't fooled. "It's the best thing to do, Karen," he said. She knew he was right. How long would she stay helpless in this cell with Queen Lavinia?

Chapter 12

Lucy dropped off some clean clothes and a pair of tiny ear-plugs so the next night in the jail cell was a bit less miserable than the first. The ear-plugs blocked Queen Lavinia's constant monologue of affirmations ("I proclaim my innocence;" and "Thoughts are things. My thoughts prevail."). Sure.

The next day was endless. Lucy's visit took only a few moments, and for the rest of the long day, Karen had novels that scarcely held her interest, punctuated by Queen Lavinia's frequent visits from her flock of admirers. What was her appeal, Karen wondered. If it was the promise of getting rich, Lavinia's followers didn't appear to have mastered the technique yet. They were a shabby lot, but maybe they were just beginners. Several of the women had imitated Lavinia's flamboyant curly hair and adopted the trademark jumbo hoop earrings she wore. The men were clearly drawn by her earthy sexuality—was this woman-power so strong that they'd go out and steal for her?

On the next day, Karen was surprised to see Curly approaching with another man in tow. A tall, black, 40-ish man, he was dressed in a dark suit and tie—in Florida's retirement paradise, most men gave up formality, even for church, so the somberly dressed man caught the eye of the prison staff and Lavinia's flock as well. Karen had expected a jovial Irishman, from the name, but Bill Daly was all business.

"I found a lawyer for you," Curly said to Karen and her audience. We can go talk privately—I secured an interview room." As the guard led Karen off behind the two men, she wondered when she'd ever attracted the notice of so many people before—maybe not since her going-away party from Microsoft. That world had never seemed further away.

The two men sat across the table from Karen on heavy wooden chairs. Curly tipped his chair back so it was resting on the two back legs, but Daly sat straight with perfect posture.

"I'm Bill Daly," the attorney said after they were settled in the interview room. He nodded at Curly. "William here has told me the story of what's happened to you, and I think we can get you out of here. There's no question of your being acquitted eventually, but right now our problem is bail."

It took Karen a moment to realize that "William" was Curly. The attorney was all business, and that meant no frivolous nicknames. He opened his briefcase and took out a slim folder.

"As you know, the judge refused to set bail because you had no family tying you to this area, and it is a capital crime you're being investigated for. Theoretically when the judge takes that step, he's committed to move quickly and your grand jury trial should come up soon. But we all know how slowly things move in Southwest Florida. You could be here for weeks."

Daly looked at the wall, as if gathering his thoughts before he spoke.

"William and I have come up with a way for you to have some family right away. This is a bit unorthodox, I'll admit," he continued, straightening the perfectly aligned papers in his folder. "What you need to do is marry William. Then you'll have family and we can proceed to reapply to the judge. I've already spoken to the judge, in fact, and told him you two were on the verge of marriage before the unfortunate incident involving Henry Sinclair."

Karen gasped. "Marry Curly!" She blushed as her throat closed and no words would come.

Curly returned his chair firmly to the floor and leaned toward Karen, laughing. "I realize it's not the most romantic proposal a girl could have, but it's a way out. We can decide later if we're really compatible or if we need to get a divorce. If you want, Mr. Daly here can draft a pre-nup…."

Karen looked at Curly with disbelief. He was absolutely serious.

"But how could we be married? There's a principle here. I can't go through with this," Karen said.

"The alternative is a few more weeks with your Looney Tunes roommate in this jail cell," Curly said. "I've got to be a better prospect than that. In fact, I'm a little hurt to be refused so abruptly."

Ignoring lawyer and guard, Curly went on. "Look, Karen, when we went out we both knew we'd seen something special in each other. I could tell you responded to me. We haven't had a chance to pursue it, to have dates, to spend time together, but we're not kids. We know who we are by now and we know the right person when we find them. Sure, I was mad when you let yourself be pushed around by Hank and Sue Ann, but we just needed time to talk. So it's not such a long shot."

Curly got out of his chair and sank to one knee in the classic proposal pose. Daly looked away from the intimate conversation, as if not to hear.

"There's nothing you want more than family—look at what lengths you went to to make a family out of your cousins—but we're 21st century people. We need to create our family. I don't mean having children, but drawing the people we love to ourselves—not just opening your door to every freeloader who wants a Florida vacation. Karen, give it a chance.

"We could have a ceremony right here in the Lee County jail, with Lucy as a witness, and you could get out. You could go home to Junior, who, incidentally, is at home—he's pretty weak but he's his old self, trying to chase his feather toy all around. He's looking for you everywhere. You could spend the nights in your own bed with your own cat while I'm off trying to find Sue Ann. Think it over."

Curly got up from the floor and stood above Karen, watching her intently. She stared at Curly and said nothing.

Daly looked at his watch. "I don't think Ms. Sinclair is going to go along with the plan, and I have another appointment, so I'll have to be leaving." He signaled the guard.

"Wait!" Karen said. "It's just such an outlandish idea. I haven't really said no, but I need time to think."

"Karen, we don't have time." Curly was using "we" again. Could she go along with this scheme and clear away the wreckage later? What alternative did she have?

"Prosperity is my God-given right!" came the chant from Lavinia's followers all the way down the hall. "My thoughts are creating prosperity right here and right now."

"O.K.," Karen said, "let's do it." She stood up and kissed Curly lightly on the cheek.

"Who's your pastor?" Daly asked.

"Pastor Olafsen at St. Paul's," Karen told him. She hoped the staid clergyman could see his way clear to this unorthodox wedding ceremony in the jail. If he understood what the real issue was, he might be willing to bend the rules.

"We'll get back to you," Daly said as he headed out of the room. Curly kissed her again, awkwardly, as he followed the attorney. Karen and the guard made their way back to the cell after they left.

"Looks like somebody's getting married," the guard said, unfortunately within earshot of Queen Lavinia.

"You're getting married, honey?" shouted Queen Lavinia. "I knew it. I was sending an aura of positive energy out to you all night long."

Karen climbed up to her upper bunk and tried to read her spy novel. She'd forgotten who all the villains were and had to start again. Anything to blot out what her life had become. Where was Sue Ann? There was no mystery about Hank's death, and Sue Ann was the key. Karen remembered how frightened Sue Ann was to tell her of Hank's cruelty, and of how obviously she stifled her anger whenever Hank ordered her to do some menial task.

The words of the spy novel made no sense. Karen read and reread the same paragraph. But her apparent absorption in her book finally made Queen Lavinia lose interest in her.

Right after the unappetizing lunch that Karen was growing used to, another visitor appeared at her cell. Pastor Olafsen, dressed in black clerical garb, stretched his hands in through the bars to grasp Karen's. They stood only a couple of feet apart, but separated by unyielding steel.

"Karen!" he said. "I just saw the news in this morning's paper, and then I had a call from Curly. I rushed here. They told me the interview rooms are full so we have to talk here."

Karen knew this meant that the nosy Lavinia would hear everything, but she was learning that there were no secrets in a jail. "That's fine," she said. "Did Curly tell you about his plan?"

"Karen, I can't go along with this scheme. Holy matrimony is a sacrament, not to be taken on to make a deal with a judge! Besides, you need three counseling sessions with me before I can consent to perform a ceremony."

Karen felt anger and frustration overriding her natural politeness. "Pastor, this is a time to be thinking about my situation, and how a Christian responds to need, not to be thinking about the rules, the rules, the rules! It's a time for the Gospel, not the Law."

"No, Karen," the pastor replied. "Breaking the church's laws to get what you want isn't Gospel, it's just expediency. I will pray for you and when this is all over, maybe you and Curly and I can sit down and talk about marriage. Not now. I'm sorry, Karen, I can't violate my own principles. Some day you'll see that I was right."

Karen had no answer for him, and he dropped her hands and turned to leave. There was no one to turn to, not even a comfortable chair to curl up into. She sobbed against the hard bars of her cell. All the years she'd been a faithful church member, and when she needed them, they let her down. Everyone speaks of the "church family," but for Karen this hadn't been a metaphor—it had been the real thing.

She felt an arm on her shoulder just as she smelled Queen Lavinia's musky perfume and heard the jangling jewelry. "I couldn't help overhear, honey," the woman said.

Karen's sobs intensified. Not only had the church she believed in for so many years let her down, but now she had to contend with this pest.

"I can marry you and that young man. I'm still licensed to perform marriages in the state of Florida, since I'm a minister of the Church of True Happiness. I may be in jail, but I haven't gone to trial yet, and I'm innocent until proven guilty. I can put on a great wedding right here in this jail. Walls and bars and locks are meaningless to spiritual people. I'll get my boys to bring me all those official papers and you'll be legally married by nightfall. Just leave it to me."

Karen could make no response but further sobs. Through her misery, she heard Lavinia talking to some of the young men who streamed in and out of the jail at all hours. Papers were eventually inspected and handed through the bars.

When Curly returned, Queen Lavinia was ready and waiting. "Karen's pastor turned her down," she informed the baffled suitor. "But I can perform the ceremony, and

I have all the official papers right here. The guard can be a witness—she doesn't have much to do."

Curly looked at Karen's red, tear-stained face. "Yes, Curly, let's do this. Later we can deal with it…if you're still sure you want to go through with it."

"Never more ready," Curly said.

"Guard! Guard!" Lavinia shouted. The bored woman at the end of the corridor put down her *People* magazine and walked to the cell. "What's this all about?"

"What's your name?" Lavinia asked.

"What do you need to know for?" the guard replied. Lavinia was busy copying from the guard's nameplate onto her sheaf of papers.

"Sonia Gilman?" Lavinia asked. "Sonia, honey, listen, we need you to witness a marriage ceremony. It's perfectly legal; see I have all these papers. Let us have the interview room for just a few minutes. You'll be the maid of honor, girl!"

Sonia stared at all three. "Nobody ever got married in this jail before."

"That doesn't mean it's illegal," Lavinia replied "Now help us out, honey, just this once. Please. These people never hurt anybody—in all this misery, they want only one thing and that's to be together. It won't cost you anything and you don't have anything better to do but read that fool magazine. Now be a friend, Sonia."

Amazingly, Sonia relented and unlocked the cell. The wedding party followed her to the interview room where Curly and Karen held hands.

"Repeat after me," Lavinia began. Karen was amazed at the stentorian tones the odd minister could assume once she took on her official role. "I am a child of God."

"I am a child of God." Karen and Curly barely whispered out the woman's words.

"Me too?" Sonia asked.

"Hush. No, I'll tell you if you have anything to say," Lavinia answered.

"I'm freely and fully expressing the power of love in my life."

The strange litany continued, with Curly and Karen repeating whatever Lavinia ordered them to say. Karen began to wonder how much affirming would be necessary before Lavinia could sign the official papers of her married state.

"Right here and right now I'm entering into happiness and prosperity."

Karen knew Lavinia would have to throw in prosperity somewhere. Finally Queen Lavinia got to the part Karen and Curly had been waiting for. "I now pronounce you husband and wife. You may kiss the bride."

Lavinia and Sonia applauded as Curly held Karen in his arms for a long kiss. Karen knew that Curly was sincere and she wondered how she had found such a rock of a man in her time of need. Love and gratitude rolled over her as she enfolded into Curly's arms.

"You going to change your name?" Sonia asked. Karen hadn't thought of this.

"How does Karen Aubusson sound to you, Curly?" she asked.

"I like it!" he answered. "Later I'll show you how to spell it."

The little wedding party exchanged hugs, and contrary to all regulations, Sonia left the three alone in the interview room. Soon she reappeared with four vending-machine Twinkies and cans of Sprite. "It's not exactly a wedding cake and champagne, but under the circumstances...." Everyone tore into the cellophane, and Curly and Karen fed each other their Twinkies as if they'd been sharing the finest wedding cake at the most elegant ceremony in the world.

Karen hoped to hear that Daly had been able to persuade the judge to release her before she had to spend another night on the hard top bunk. Her thoughts turned to Junior and how she longed to hold him and encourage him back to health. But the wheels of justice turned too slowly and it wasn't till the following morning that the new Mrs. Aubusson was released. She exchanged hugs and tears with her new friend, Queen Lavinia, and patently false promises to keep in touch.

Her condo apartment had never looked so good. She found Junior curled up on her bed and she picked him up and listened to his loud purr. She knew he would be all right as soon as his fur closed over the ugly shaved patch. Curly kissed her goodbye with the cat in her arms.

"I won't come back without Sue Ann," he promised.

"Just come back," she replied.

She settled down to a long afternoon of petting Junior and talking to him. Occasionally she nodded off in her chair and felt the peace of her quiet home envelop them both.

Chapter 13

Afternoon faded into evening as Karen sat peacefully on her sofa listening to Junior's loud and steady purr. She assured herself that he would make a full recovery—she only hoped his memory of Kaiser's attack would fade. She hadn't heard whether Kaiser had been rescued or if he'd met the fate he deserved, but she didn't care as long as she never saw the vicious dog again.

As she relished the quiet, she drove the echoes of the clanging, noisy jail cell out of her mind. She lived over the events of the last remarkable week, thinking what a Christmas newsletter this would make. "Dear Friends, Three men died horribly when visiting me, but now I'm happily married so it all worked out in the end. I hope the New Year brings you every blessing...."

What would she do about her marriage to Curly? Of course on one level it was just an expedient to get her out of jail, and if all she had was this quiet evening, it was well worth it. A divorce wouldn't be that hard to get—maybe even an annulment. But did he mean his words? Had they really found the right person to start over with? Should she give up the life she'd come to treasure as her own woman, with her own time, her own schedule, her own values? Were she and Curly so mature and experienced that they could recognize love when it came, without the long courtship tradition demanded? Had they both learned something of value from the failure of their first marriages? Did they really not need "world enough and time?"

The doorbell jolted Karen out of her thoughts. She realized it had gotten dark—it was now almost 8:00 and she certainly wasn't expecting anyone. Lucy maybe? She gently dislodged Junior and went to the door to look through the peephole.

There was Hank.

She froze. Hank was dead! But had she actually seen Hank die? No! She'd only heard from the coroner that he was dead. She told Hank never to come near her home again and here he was, only he was dead. But he wasn't dead. She was losing her grip.

"Karen, please, let us in!" came the plea from the other side of the door.

She took another look through the peephole to see Sue Ann standing beside Hank. Yielding to curiosity, she pushed her horror aside, released the door chain, and slid open the deadlock.

"Karen, I know I shouldn't have come," Sue Ann began, "but this is my son Wayne—he came down here for me—and we decided we needed to talk to you first."

"Sue Ann, he looks exactly like his father. I thought Hank had come back!" Karen gasped.

"I know, everybody always told him that. His brother Paulie looks the same. Didn't we show you pictures when we was here?" Sue Ann asked.

"I don't remember, but you gave me a scare. I thought Hank had come back."

Now Sue Ann broke down. Wayne put his arm around her shoulders.

By now Junior was cautiously hidden under the bed in Karen's room and the sofa was empty. Karen belatedly asked Sue Ann and Wayne to come in and sit down.

Sue Ann sat on the edge of the sofa, as if not to disturb it. Wayne joined her and took her hand as she spoke.

"I know I should have come sooner," Sue Ann said. "By the time Wayne got down here, you were already in jail. I knew about it from the papers. I didn't know what to do. I couldn't let you take the blame for what I did, but I was so afraid. I kept thinking about the electric chair or whatever they do to people in Florida. I was afraid.

"I killed him," she went on, wiping her eyes as she spoke. "Of course you knew I must have. Remember that day we had lunch and you said I shouldn't take it when Hank hit me? I was thinking and thinking about that. I saw how good you had it living alone and I wanted that life. And I was sick of Hank ordering me around all day long."

Wayne released Sue Ann's hand as she reached into her purse for more tissues. For a few moments, she couldn't speak. Karen waited for her to continue.

"When we left here, Hank was really mad," she said as soon as she'd gotten her voice back. "He drove crazy, finally stopped at the gas station by the freeway ramp. After he filled up, he pulled over in that construction site where they're building the Home Depot, and just sat in the truck. He was mad at Kaiser, and you can understand that. He beat up on the dog some—I know that's why the dog is as mean as he is. But then he started in on me, how it was all my fault, how I should have kept the dog away from the cat, and why didn't I have control of the dog."

Karen shuddered, remembering the brutality of the enormous dog.

"I thought, 'why is that my fault? I never liked the damn dog, you brought him home without asking me anything about it and I'm the one has to take care of him, and it's not my fault that he's mean and got out of control.' So I hit Hank back—I slapped him in the face. I've never done that before. I usually just try to cover myself up. He was so surprised it took him a minute before he started in on me again—he was hitting me in the head and on my neck and I slumped onto the floor of the truck. That's where I saw that long knife he bought at Wal-Mart that time—just laying on the floor of the truck."

Wayne took his mother's hand once again.

"It was wrong, what I did next. But you don't exactly think things over when somebody's beating on you. I picked the thing up and sort of waved it around—I couldn't see too good—and it hit him in the neck—he wasn't wearing but a t-shirt so he didn't have a collar in the way.

"I never saw so much blood come out of anybody. I've never been so scared in my life. Later on I remembered all the things that woman said about that knife at Wal-Mart. How the edge of it would cut anything. It didn't seem like I pressed on it at all and it cut right into him. I mean I didn't really stab him, like the papers said; it was just sort of an accident that the knife went into his neck. I know that doesn't make sense."

Sue Ann gave in to renewed sobs. Wayne patted her shoulder comfortingly until she composed herself and continued.

"I'd give anything to take it back. I didn't want to kill him, just to make him stop. But it wasn't long before I could see that that's what I'd done—I killed him. He didn't say a word. He wasn't breathing any more. I grabbed my coat from the back—even though it was a hot night—it covered up all the blood on me—and my purse. Then I thought I needed some money, so I reached into Hank's jeans and got out his wallet.

"It was horrible touching him, even reaching into his jeans. The dog was yapping and Hank was dead or at least dying and I didn't know what to do."

Wayne and Karen listened raptly while Sue Ann went on with her gruesome story.

"So I walked to the Days Inn Motel over there by the freeway and took a room, calm as if nothing had happened. I don't know what came over me. I wrote my maiden name, Susan Pelleteri, and paid with cash, so nobody asked me any questions. I kind of think I'm not a person people pay too much notice to. I called Wayne and he drove all the way down here."

Wayne smiled at his mother and cracked his knuckles.

"While I was waiting in the motel, I wanted to call you but I didn't know what to say. I read the paper every morning and I knew you were in trouble for what I did, but I couldn't think of what to do. Wayne got here on Wednesday and we still didn't do anything for a while.

"I'm not proud of this but I thought about leaving things the way they were. I was so scared, I thought Karen's smart, she can handle this better than I could. But I couldn't sleep with that idea."

Sue Ann got up and walked to the window with her back to Karen. "I can't face you when I tell you this, but when we came here, Hank wanted to take advantage of you. He figured out you were single and didn't have no children, so he thought he'd make up to you so you'd leave everything to our kids. That's why he kept going on about family, family. I don't think it's really family if you haven't laid eyes on each other in 35 years, but he thought he could sweet-talk you into sort of adopting our boys as your own nephews and leave them a lot of money some day."

"I understand," Karen said. "I have a lot of friends with children who have the same idea. A single woman with some savings looks like a walking gold mine to some people."

Sue Ann came back to the sofa. "When Wayne read that you'd been released, he said, 'Mama, we've got to go talk to this woman.' He's right. So here I am. You can call the police any time. I'm ready."

Perhaps drawn by Sue Ann's soft voice, Junior gingerly put his head around the corner into the living room.

"Junior's OK!" Sue Ann said. "I thought he'd be dead! I kept picturing him when you put him in that carrier and we took him to the vet. I didn't think he had a chance."

Seeing the little cat, who had been through so much fear and pain, Karen exploded. "Junior survived. Kaiser had ripped open his chest and he couldn't breathe on his own, but the vet put a tube in there to breathe for him until he healed. I didn't know if he'd live or die."

Junior saw Wayne and retreated back to the bedroom. Karen couldn't stop now that she'd begun to let her feelings out. Her voice rose and she stood and crossed her arms. "So all this time you've been only five miles away, sleeping in the Days Inn Motel while I slept—or didn't sleep—on a bunk in a jail cell with a bunch of crazies, noise all night long—you ate whatever you pleased while I ate stale sandwiches and cold coffee. And you didn't even step forward. You were too craven to admit what happened. I was afraid I'd be convicted of killing Hank when I was innocent. Can you imagine what that fear is like? You had no right to leave me hanging."

"I'm not proud of it," Sue Ann said.

Wayne stood and finally spoke up. "My mother was scared to death. I personally think she can explain what happened and it's going to be self-defense so I think she's going to be OK. But she's scared. She's never even had a traffic ticket in her life."

Karen melted a little—she tried to picture the life Sue Ann had been leading, bullied and brutalized for years and years, and when she finally fights back for the first time, she commits a murder. How she had probably wished for Hank to die all those years and then she killed him, to her own surprise, and as a perverse wish fulfillment.

"You will have to go to the police. But there's no point going tonight—you can stay here one night and have your last good night's sleep for a while—we can go forth in the morning."

Sue Ann, ever procrastinating from the horror she saw before her, agreed quickly. The two women bustled about making up beds. Sue Ann and Wayne seemed to be comfortable sharing the guest room with its twin beds. Karen finally left them and went to her own room. She climbed into bed, but it was a long time before she could close her eyes. She marveled at what wreckage had come from her simple desire to have a family of her own.

As she and Junior settled to sleep, she prayed for guidance. She wondered if she hadn't had it all along.

Chapter 14

The next morning Wayne and Sue Ann were up early. Karen made breakfast, ever the hostess, and the three of them drove off in two cars to face what they had to face.

At the now-familiar station, the efficient Sgt. Hoff took Sue Ann away for the confession and booking; Karen managed to call Bill Daly's office and secure his services to defend Sue Ann. To her surprise he responded quickly. He refused to speculate on the validity of the self-defense plea, based on Karen's quick sketch of events, but at least he didn't rule it out. Perhaps he was intrigued by the unusual case. She left everything in his capable hands, and said goodbye to Wayne, who was going to stay with his mother as long as he could. Karen wondered if Sue Ann would share a cell with the redoubtable Queen Lavinia.

Thinking she was finally free, she was surprised to face a couple of reporters as she left the courthouse. "No comment, no comment!" she said as she'd seen crooked CEOs and politicians do on TV. "No comment on any aspect of this case!"

She drove by Lucy's apartment, delighted to find her friend at home and possessed of a couple of free hours. Sheets of music were spread out all over the baby grand piano.

"I have a job singing at a wedding!" Lucy announced. "I'm trying to find something better than 'O Promise Me.'"

"How about "Love is wonderful, the second time around?" Karen asked. She sat down over a pot of tea to tell the whole remarkable story.

"Let's start by telling you that I got married. My maid-of-honor was a prison guard, but I'd have preferred you!"

For the first time in their long and intimate friendship, Lucy was without words. Karen continued through the courthouse drama, the impromptu wedding, and Curly's departure.

"So I'm a married woman, and I don't know when I'm going to see my new husband again. He's off in New Jersey tracking down Sue Ann," Karen concluded.

"Karen, nobody but me would believe this story if you told them," Lucy said. "Let's hide out on the beach and soak up some Florida sunshine. I'll bet jail time gives you a Vitamin D deficiency in the worst way.

"Great idea," Karen replied. "I'll meet you at Barefoot Beach in an hour."

Karen checked on Junior again. He was snoozing comfortably in the middle of Karen's bed, so she though it would be safe to leave him for a few hours. She packed up her beach gear. Usually she was ready at a moment's notice to go to the beach, but now she had to take a while to make sure her bag held sunblock, reading material, sunglasses, and beach towel, and assemble all the familiar accessories.

Never had she appreciated the pristine Gulf Coast beach so much as that day. Like most year-round Floridians, she found the water too cool to swim in until at least June or July, but she waded, picked up shells, scanned the water for dolphins, dozed in the sun, and ingested the peace and calm that only a wide ocean horizon can bring. Her problems seemed less formidable and her future more hopeful by the time she and Lucy folded their beach chairs and headed home.

* * * *

After her day of "solar therapy," she holed up in her apartment and hovered by the phone, one ear tuned to the doorbell. Surely Curly would show up or call. She wondered if there were some way she could find Wayne's brother Paul in New Jersey just in case Curly contacted him. She schemed for ways to make contact with him. Having always scorned the people she saw attached to their cell phones, she wished Curly had one now. She calculated that south Jersey was a hard two days' drive from the southwestern tip of Florida. Her imagination conjured up flat tires, flooded roads, and hostility from Paul.

Three more nights went by, each one longer than the last. Junior seemed to be glad to have Karen's undivided attention, but she was growing more and more concerned. If anything happened to Curly, who would know enough to call his…well, his wife? She tried all the amusements she knew of without leaving her home—she read, she sewed, she watched too much TV, and she cooked exotic dishes for herself. She managed not to binge on anything forbidden in spite of her anxiety. Lucy came over one evening to run through her wedding song for Karen and Junior, and the two played Scrabble till they were both tired enough to call it a night.

By the time the doorbell finally rang, Karen flew to open it without even checking the peephole. She knew it would be Curly, and she threw herself into his arms.

"I can't find them, Karen. I know I promised not to come back without Sue Ann, but she's disappeared from the earth. I found her son Paul, but he wouldn't even talk to me. I was pretty sure he was hiding something, but even when I followed him around, he didn't lead me to anything. The address where Sue Ann and Hank lived is shut up tight. Nobody's been there for a long time. The neighbors—"

Karen began to laugh, not the reaction Curly had expected. "Let me fix you a stiff drink and tell you a story," she said.

"Scotch, neat, no ice, no water," he said.

As he sipped his drink, she told him about Sue Ann's appearance at her door such a short time after Curly had left Florida, and the quick resolution of all Karen's anxiety about her own future as a criminal. Finally she went to the kitchen to rinse their glasses. "If you'd stayed here for a proper wedding night, I could have saved you the trip to New Jersey," Karen said, surprised at her own boldness.

"Any chance we can make up for that?" Curly asked, moving behind her and kissing the back of her neck gently.

Karen turned to face him and fold herself into his arms. She returned his kiss and felt that sudden certain knowledge that this was right. However crazily they had come together, they belonged together.

Karen expected their first time to be all awkward elbows and misconnections and clumsy fumblings. But they seemed to melt into each other' arms. Curly led her into the bedroom, somehow nudging Junior to the far corner of the bed. They slipped off each other's t-shirts and explored each other's bodies at a tantalizing pace. Although Curly appeared to be lean, his body was hardened by outdoor work,

They knew at the same moment that they could wait no longer. Tearing off what was left of their clothes, they wriggled under the bedspread and found each other, wringing passion out of all the desire and confusion and pain of the short time they'd had together.

As they subsided to a comfortable married embrace and drifted off toward sleep, Karen thought again of the old song, "Love is wonderful, the second time around." Junior climbed up onto Curly's feet and went back to sleep, his small blessing on their union.

The next morning the phone awakened Karen and Curly. Karen woke slowly, the warmth and pleasure of the previous night still in her heart. "Hello," she answered, turning her back to Curly.

"Karen? This is Anne. You know, Anne Capra."

Anne, Anne, Anne. Karen searched her memory. Nothing came up.

"We worked on that help system together, remember, back on the World War II strategy game at Microsoft?"

"Oh yes," Karen answered, finally remembering a short, dark-haired writer whose command of English grammar had needed a full remedial course, but who knew everything there was to know about German tanks, making her invaluable for the game they were documenting. "How are you, Anne?"

By now Curly was awake and watching Karen's end of the conversation. He stroked her neck and shoulders, distracting her utterly from her conversation.

"Well, Karen, I'm just fine, and we finally shipped War Game Mania, so I have some free time coming up.

It's been really cold and dark and rainy up here, so I couldn't help thinking of you in Florida."

Karen sat upright, as a singer does when preparing her diaphragm for a demanding aria. "Anne, I know what you're going to ask. I have a lot of guests here, and I just can't accommodate any more in my home. I'm sorry. I'll be glad to find you a hotel—there are a lot on the beach that you'd find very comfortable, but my apartment just isn't available."

Curly gave a loud stadium whistle and applauded. Junior pounced on Curly's stomach.

Karen clapped a hand over the receiver and fell back onto the pillow laughing.

* * * *

The Wonder Gardens had never been the scene of a wedding reception before, but the owner was willing to close down early for an afternoon in this very special case. Curly had not mentioned to the tuxedo-rental shop just where he planned to wear the dashing suit he chose. Karen decked herself out in a short version of a traditional gown, and talked Lucy into a fluffy pink bridesmaid dress.

Karen asked Wayne Sinclair to be among the guests, and he told them privately that he had high hopes that Daly's self-defense plea would be successful. He seemed to be in good spirits, and he was showing more than a little interest in one of the new receptionists from the front desk.

Lucy sang what was now Karen's favorite song, "Love is wonderful, the second time around." Karen found tears in her eyes, which Curly gently wiped away. To follow the song, the peacocks screamed, the boars snorted, and the geese honked, knowing this wasn't an ordinary day at the Wonder Gardens.

The couple led the wedding party all the way around the park, stopping to feed the deer and the turtles, offering a couple of dog biscuits to the bears, Luke and Slewfoot, passing quickly by the crocodile enclosure, and walking calmly on the rickety swinging bridge that overlooked the alligators. They toasted each other and all their guests beside Big Joe, the 14 ½ foot crocodile. They sliced wedding cake in front of Mort the Otter, who ran up the ladder and flew down his slide to show his joy.

About the Author

Merle Barbara Metcalfe retired early from Microsoft where she'd been Director of User Education. After Seattle, she was looking for sunshine—and she found it in southwest Florida. She didn't realize that she'd be deluged with houseguests once she settled near the beach.

From this experience, she imagined her book, Freeloaders, about a similar young retiree, Karen Sinclair, but Karen's guests started to die in spectacular ways— this may have been catharsis, but it was certainly funny. And the feel-good ending was a hit with early readers.

Metcalfe brings 30 years of writing experience to the task—award-winning software manuals, theater reviews, and magazine articles—but this is her first novel.

Printed in the United States
50414LVS00001B/274-417